打开星星的光芒
Unveiling the Star's Light

强爱香 / 著　马燕 / 译

Written by Qiang Aixiang

Translated by Julie Yan Ma

北京燕山出版社

图书在版编目（CIP）数据

　　打开星星的光芒：汉英对照/强爱香著，马燕译．——北京：北京燕山出版社，2016.12
　　ISBN 978-7-5402-4381-4

　　Ⅰ．①打… Ⅱ．①强… ②马… Ⅲ．①诗集—中国—当代—汉、英 Ⅳ．① I227

中国版本图书馆 CIP 数据核字 (2017) 第 003781 号

打开星星的光芒

作　　　者：	强爱香
译　　　者：	马　燕
责　　编：	郭东梅
责任校对：	甄　飞　岳　欣
封面设计：	山水悟道文化工作室
社　　　址：	北京市西城区陶然亭路 53 号（100054）
网　　　站：	http://www.bjyspress.com/
微　　　博：	http://weibo.com/u/2526206071
电　　　话：	01065240430
传　　　真：	01063587071
印　　　刷：	廊坊市燕京安全印务有限公司
开　　　本：	880mm×1230mm 1/32
字　　　数：	180 千字
印　　　张：	9
版　　　次：	2017 年 4 月第 1 版
印　　　次：	2017 年 4 月第 1 次印刷
定　　　价：	36.80 元
出版发行：	北京燕山出版社

版权所有　翻版必究

目 录
CONTENTS

上部

第一辑　遥远的歌声

- 003　琴音
- 005　遥远的歌声
- 007　站在河边
- 009　在小小的船上
- 011　沉静的月影
- 013　我不敢说
- 015　悄悄的夜雨
- 017　泊月
- 019　黑夜里的泥土
- 021　六月的海
- 023　蝶翅上的六月

第二辑　安静的村庄

- **027**　家
- **029**　小路
- **031**　小花
- **033**　兰花
- **035**　桃花
- **037**　搬运春天的蜜蜂
- **039**　安静的村庄
- **041**　早晨的露滴
- **043**　一地槐花
- **045**　夜晚升起在唇沿
- **047**　橘子的月亮
- **049**　我的窗含满星光
- **051**　深夜

第三辑　我看见秋天了

- 055　看见大片的野菊
- 057　露滴
- 059　我看见秋天了
- 061　秋天的爱情
- 063　搬运秋天的蚂蚁
- 065　秋菊
- 067　秋水
- 069　一叶秋风
- 071　秋风吹进我内心
- 073　几片卷曲的落叶
- 075　秋天的抒情
- 079　走进秋天的腹地

第四辑　春天的声音

- 083　一片叶子
- 085　我以一朵花的姿势开放
- 087　有一种飞都有蝴蝶的内心
- 089　我是岛上的一只蝴蝶
- 091　鸥鸟
- 093　我听见了什么
- 095　开放
- 097　溪边的一棵小草
- 099　春风拂过来
- 101　春晚如花
- 103　小竹林
- 105　夜
- 107　一抹夕阳
- 109　月亮的花瓣

下部

第一辑　雨季之外

113　一个梦
117　燃烧的花瓣
121　风中的菊花
123　一株草黄了
125　叶子的自语
127　岸上的影子
129　失踪
131　钥匙
133　秋风早晨
135　中秋月
137　树梢上的月亮
139　秋雁
141　我坐下来，秋天高高在上
145　一只鸟飞出静夜
147　一只翅膀飞过泥泞
149　我也是一枚种子
151　小路上的脚印
153　且行且远

第二辑　冬天的河流

- 157　河床
- 159　冰河
- 161　暗流
- 163　夜之风
- 165　流凌
- 167　黑夜正塌陷下来
- 169　风不知道往哪边吹
- 171　而我,依然擎着一枚火把
- 173　走吧——
- 175　冰的行走方式
- 177　河流的目光
- 181　没有冻伤的鸟鸣
- 183　开在寒风中的花
- 185　一汪静水
- 189　独坐江岸
- 193　我的沉思被一块石头占有

第三辑　雪落有声

- 199　一盏太阳的橘灯
- 201　打开冬天的记忆
- 203　雪落有声
- 205　雪的重量
- 207　雪域
- 209　雪的背后是湿地
- 211　雪花　一瓣瓣月光
- 213　树上盛开着雪意
- 215　一处草地被一场雪释解
- 217　雪影

第四辑　打开星星的光芒

221　那片海
223　象征
225　走进一滴雨
227　水边的舞蹈
231　独占的旷野
235　与诗有关
251　举起你的手来
255　你无法走进纯净的时间
257　打开星星的光芒
261　打开台灯，静静把世界放下来

PART 1 Songs from Faraway

004   Sound of an Instrument
006   Songs from Faraway
008   Standing by the River
010   In a Petit Boat
012   Shadow of the Moon
014   I Dare Not Say
016   Stealthy Night Rain
018   Pallid Moon
020   Sailing Through a Dark Night
022   Ocean of June
024   June on Butterfly Wings

目录

PART 2 A Peacefull Village

028	Home
030	On This Path
032	Small Flowers
034	Orchid
036	Peach Blossom
038	Spring Carried by the Bees
040	A Peacefull Village
042	Morning Dewdrops
044	Locust Flowers
046	Night Rising
048	Tangerine Moon
050	My Window Full with Starlight
052	Late at Night

PART 3 I See the Autumn

- **056** A Great Stretch of Chrysanthemum Field
- **058** Dewdrops
- **060** I See the Autumn
- **062** Autumn Love
- **064** Ants Carrying the Fall
- **066** Autumn Chrysanthemum
- **068** Autumn Water
- **070** Autumn Breeze
- **072** Autumn Wind Blowing into My Heart
- **074** A few Curled Leaves
- **077** A Love Song for the Fall
- **080** Walking on Autumn's Hinterland

目录

PART 4 Sound of the Spring

084	A Leaf
086	Blooming Like a Flower
088	A Butterfly's Soul
090	A Butterfly on an Island
092	Gulls
094	I Hear
096	In Full Bloom
098	Grass by a Greek
100	Spring Breeze
102	Spring Night Blossom
104	Little Bamboo Forest
106	Night
108	Sunset
110	Petals of the Moon

CONTENTS

PART 1 After the Monsoon

115	A Dream
119	Flaming Petals
122	Chrysanthemum in the Wind
124	A Withered Grass
126	A Leaf's Soliloquy
128	Shadows over the River Bank
130	Lost
132	Keys
134	Morning Wind in the Fall
136	Mid-autumn Moon
138	Moon Clipping the Tree
140	Autumn Geese
143	Under the High Autumn Sky
146	A Bird Flies Away on a Tranquil Night
148	A Wing Flying over a Muddy Field
150	A Seed
152	Footprints on a Trail
154	Journey as We Continue

PART 2 Rivers in the Winter

158	Riverbed
160	Glacier
162	Undercurrent
164	Nightly Wind
166	Ice Run
168	Dark Night Falling
170	Which Way the Wind Is Blowing
172	Holding up a Torch
174	Let's Go
176	How Ice Walks
179	Gaze of a River
182	Bird's Chirping Unharmed
184	Flowers Blooming in Chilly Wind
187	A Pond of Still Water
191	Loner by the River Bank
196	Thoughts Seized by a Stone

PART 3 Sound of Snow Falling

- **200**   The Orange Light of the Sun
- **202**   Awaken Winter's Memories
- **204**   Sound of Snow Falling
- **206**   Weight of the Snow
- **208**   Snow Field
- **210**   Wetland Behind the Snow
- **212**   Snowflakes, Petals of the Moon
- **214**   Snow Perching on the Tree
- **216**   A Lawn Interpreted by Snow
- **218**   Shadow of the Snow

PART 4 Unveiling the Star's Light

222	This Ocean
224	Symbols
226	Walking into a Drop of Rain
229	A Dance by the Water
233	Wilderness Field
236	Concerning Poetry
253	Raise Your Hand
256	Unable to Enter Pure Time
259	Unveiling the Star's Light
263	Turn on the Lamp, and Turn off the World

上部

第一辑　遥远的歌声
PART 1 Songs from Faraway

打开星星的光芒

琴音

那是谁的声音
让我想象到一个遥远
那是谁轻轻的脚步
踩着月光推开另一扇门

琴音是什么颜色的
让我托着天空想着星星
我听着听着就陷了下去
就像是一个黑夜的样子
我沉静在音节上看见自己的忧愁

Unveiling the Star's Light

Sound of an Instrument

Whose voice is that charming tune
Calling me to a distant home
Stepping on the soft moonlight
Pushing another door

What color shines in the music?
The key that ascends to stars above
Fallilg on me at a decrescendo
A dark night plays melancholy on the scales

打开星星的光芒

遥远的歌声

遥远的歌声曾飘过妈妈的背影
就像清晨的炊烟写着村庄的温暖
这些歌声生长在玉米地里
生长在妈妈的手心
这些歌声生长在老街的墙上
有一张猜不透的脸

遥远的歌声漂染我的青春
我驻足在每个词语上生动
我是飞临大海的鸟
我要把歌声种植在蓝天

Unveiling the Star's Light

Songs from Faraway

A song from faraway carries a mother's weight
When morning fog warms village
Old tunes grew wings in corn fields
Inside the palms of a mother's hands
They cling to walls along a cobblestone street
Drawing an indescribable face

Faraway songs dig in memory of youth
Lingering at each word
I am a bird hovering over the ocean
Screeching an old tune over and over

打开星星的光芒

站在河边

此时,我就是云了
我行走在水里
我摸到体内的鱼群
这些小小的幸福像花朵般盛开
此时,我幸福得沉默
看着河岸弯过果园
弯过一座村庄的背影

站在河边
背靠巨大天空的石子
我穿过石子上的光
穿过秋天在一棵树木上的思考
我就是云了
我要摸到河流的秘密

Unveiling the Star's Light

Standing by the River

Now I become a cloud
A cIoud walking in the water
Feeling fish swarming inside
Happiness bursts into blossoms
A moment of silent complacence
I watch a river bank the orchard
Reaching to the back of my village

By the river against a stone I stand
A giant stone against the vast sky
I shall pass through the light of the stone
Through thoughts of autumn in the trees
And I shall become that cloud in the water
Searching for the river's secrets

打开星星的光芒

在小小的船上

我在小小的船上看着水
鱼和水草如此静美
我在船上划着水
水一圈圈扩展,水扭曲了我
日光拉长了我的手臂
我在水里像忧郁的浮萍

我所能做的就是到达彼岸
彼岸上有羊群咀嚼
有一些陌生的树木挂着夕阳
还有一些等待的事物,都与我有关

Unveiling the Star's Light

In a Petit Boat

In this petit boat I watch the water flow
Fish and water weeds calm and beautiful
I waddle through
Ripples circle and distort
Sun stretches my arms and hands
A lone duckweed floats

I only wish to reach the shore
Where sheep are grazing on green hills
The setting sun is hanging on a tall tree
And mysteries unfold

打开星星的光芒

沉静的月影

夏蝉最终没有串起来
就像串不起的思绪
这些移动在墙上的月影
铺展在小路上的月影

是碎了的心事被风轻轻地摇
夜晚更深了
我解不破这一地的沉静
这些慢慢爬上额际的月影
让我找不到最初的睡眠
这些小小的阴郁比一次忧愁还生动
它们几乎都张着小小的手,要递给我什么

Shadow of the Moon

Cicada's wings too brittle to string
Like thoughts that can't be strung together
Shadow of the moon travels on a wall
And over a tiny path, it slowly crawls

Broken hearts consoled by soothing wind
Night is getting deeper and thin
Impenetrable shades cling onto my forehead
As I find peace, but lose my sleep
Such vivid shadows overcome melancholy
A hand reaches over to pass me something

我不敢说

我始终没能说出
像说不出一个海的蓝
我最终还是站在海的边沿
在一个雨后的下午
我理解了一朵花上的蚂蚁
蚂蚁是在咬着我的心吗

我不敢说
就像不敢把目光再深入到一个点
而内心的潮，涨在什么位置
我不敢说
是否还有一个人从此悄悄走过

I Dare Not Say

I fail to say a word
As I can't tell about ocean's blue
So I stand by the sea after the rain
I onesome on this afternoon
Apprehensive about ants on a flower
Its core a heart being nibbled on

I dare not say
As I no longer stare into a burning dot
The cycle of tides rises and falls
I dare not imagine
That you'd come by this moment
And walk away without saying a word

打开星星的光芒

悄悄的夜雨

你在敲打着谁的窗户
然后放进脚步　让我看见你的神情
你默默地走进街道和一片黑暗里的尘事
然后不住地张望　你要等待着谁

你悄悄地脱掉季节带来的沉重
在许多人未梦见你之前
在一片原野将空出来的时候
或许那些细密的手指　要戳破最后的故事

Unveiling the Star's Light

Stealthy Night Rain

You knock on the window
Seeping through sill
Showing a curious face
You run on streets and over darkness
Who are you waiting for, always hurried?

Stealthily you unload the burden from the season
And you reappear in dreams
The hinterland awaits your arrival
But those dense thin fingers
Still poking
For the last conspiracy

打开星星的光芒

泊月

这天晚上全家人都围着它
全家的全家人都围着它
我用纸裁剪　用酒醉　用私语塞它
最后我走在被草装饰的小路上
在我沉默的时候
它跳上了草尖　是一颗露滴
它打湿了我的脚尖
这个时候　我的影子很长很长
河水流过我身体的中央
月光一片片　碎了一地思念

深夜　我收获了安静
安静也是一枚火焰
我的火焰照着城市的墙
我要推开它抵达月亮的后花园
那上面的阴影是谁丢掉的衣裳
那轮弯月是谁的脊梁
那是一个最模糊的轮廓
是谁常年地跪拜与祈求
今天深夜　我悄悄收藏

Unveiling the Star's Light

Pallid Moon

Tonight it will be surrounded
The entire family will be surrounding the moon
I use cut paper, liquor and secret signs
To stuff it to the perfect roundness
Then I shall walk on a road draped with evergreens
Jump on grass tips, and my toes get wet
My shadow elongated to match the length of the road
A river runs through it
With reflections under melancholic moonlight

I shall harvest the midnight's tranquility
Stillness in white flames
lighting the walls of the city
I shall knock down these walls
And crawl inside to the moonlight garden
Pieces of clothes hang like shadowy curtains
There I shall see, crescent like a curvy backbone
Behind that blurry contour a prayer with bended knees
Tonight, I listen carefully to the voices

打开星星的光芒

黑夜里的泥土

我还不能进入
只是在泥土的边沿听那些虫鸣
叫出一个季节的内涵

是的,我走不进去
不是因为有黑夜的栅栏
而是我没有读出沉埋的历史
那些匍匐在地的人,寂寞者
那些孤独的歌者还沉埋在风里

这个时候,我转不过身来
我怕着那些虫鸣弹完悠古
我怕着失去黑夜里的光亮

Unveiling the Star's Light

Sailing Through a Dark Night

A space I cannot enter
Only to hear sounds of insects hovering
Vivid details of the season

The soil is a space I can't hide in
And not for the night barrier
As I am blind to the buried, the unknown
Those crawling inside, loners they must have been
Their songs permeate the ground cover

I shall not turn back
Fearing the bugs would finish their tunes, and
Fearing that I might lose light in the dark

六月的海

六月就是一座海
我坐着太阳的船穿过
我看到花朵的旋涡,树木支撑的海脊
我看到鸟赶着海,海在深夜沿着大地的梦攀爬
我看到许多声音也落下来,像海上燃烧的彩霞

这个时候,我感到了一个海的质感
一个海在六月的城市,村庄以及天上
一个说不清的涌荡被雨水一次次带向远方
六月的海,是绿色染成的
是看不见的颜色染成的,像我的一个夜晚
我漂在海上,感到是有另一个海在涌着它

Unveiling the Star's Light

Ocean of June

June is an ocean caught in flames
I sail through it in the sun's ship
Whirlpools of flowers, trees stretching their limbs
Birds chasing waves
Waves chasing dreams

I see hefty sounds rise and fall
Clouds burning to ashes
I breathe in ocean's substance and my sustenance
It oversees celestial trellis, cities and villages
Rains taking torrents to faraway eternity
Ocean of June in shades of evergreen
Boiling in pots of invisible colors
And this night I float in
The sea is swelling and pushed by another sea

打开星星的光芒

蝶翅上的六月

是一幅小小的油画
款款展开麦地上的麦芒和雨水的后方
村庄和一口井谈出秘密
渺小的远　起伏于蝶翅
一处小小的粮田正被一个词语解放
这是叶帆蜂拥成的海
那些浪冲击着天空的出口
这个海独有的影子从土地目光里流出来
这么宽大的绿色胜过夜晚的深度
一次奔放似乎解开所有生命的矛盾
我们守住了每个早晨　想象梦的鱼群

这是蝶翅上的六月
我们是鸥鸟
我们舞蹈在绿色的声音里
在风掀开的背面深入生活
我看到的美是一个草帽下的少女
少女与一条流淌的溪水
我看到的美是金黄色的道路飘满的生命
是一棵树挽着另一棵树
它们在花正走过的地方留住一处蓝天
它们这些都在小小蝶翅上　不知像谁的手掌

Unveiling the Star's Light

June on Butterfly Wings

A small oil paining
Unfolding itself above wheat fields after the rain
The village is confiding its secret to a deep well
Distant voices rise and fall like butterfly wings
Patches of fields freed by words
This is an ocean packed with sails
Waves pushing to exit the sky
Lonesome shadows loom in earth's gaze
Spectrum of green deepens the night
And letting go would remove restraints
We guard each morning with care, and
Envision schools of fish

This is June on butterfly wings
We are gulls dancing to green voices
Deep woods unveiled by the wind
Beauty is a girl's straw-hat face
A stream quietly passing through
I see beauty on a golden path with living creatures
Two trees holding hands, flowers strolling by
Patch of blue sky shines in divinity
All riding on tiny butterfly wings, and wings shape like
Invisible hands

第二辑 安静的村庄

PART 2 A Peacefull Village

打开星星的光芒

家

一开始
我的家是一枚小小的茧
里面住着我的爱人

春天来了
我的爱人是一只蝴蝶
把我的家搬到一朵花里
我就在一朵花里
看着爱人的翅膀

Home

From the start
My home is a small cocoon
Inside lives my love

Spring turns my love into a butterfly
So I move our home inside a flower
And I see the wings

打开星星的光芒

小路

这是我经常走过的
上面有我的脚印
上面只有我想一个人的样子
只有几滴鸟鸣散着我的内心

亲切的小路　载着我的背影
小小的孤独　叶子遮不住
只有一个人的话语　像一把伞
只有我在想他的时候　下雨

On This Path

Often I walk on this path
Leaving countless footprints
And images of someone dear
Thoughts only interrupted by birds singing

A familiar path, carrying the shadow of my back
Dense leaves fail to hide my loneliness
And your voice is the umbrella
Whenever I yearn, it begins to rain

打开星星的光芒

小花

这些被风忽略的小小火焰
在寂寞的地方燃烧
它们走在一条细瘦的路上
在阴影里弯曲

它们没有名字
抓住一丝光亮就怒放
它们最先接触到黑暗
在最潮湿的地方举着小小灯火

Small Flowers

These little flames are neglected by the wind
Burning in solitude
They walk on a narrow path
Hunched over in their shadows

With unknown names
They reach for possible light and photosynthesize
Unafraid of darkness
They raise lanterns over the wetland

打开星星的光芒

兰花

小小的兰花在荫里
这干净的精灵在轻轻吟唱
她唱在尘埃落地的地方
她唱在一束光走过的地方

兰花　缄默不语
我看不见你的死亡
看不见你行走的方向
我感到了你的纯洁　悄悄对着远方

Unveiling the Star's Light

Orchid

Quiet and shadowed
Purple fairy hums a soft lullaby
Where dusts fall
Where light travels through

There is a part of you that's kept silent
With you on this path that has no end
Though unaware of your destiny
I feel the pureness, and it resonates

桃花

桃花　我看见你时我在暗处
桃花　我看见你时我在水边照着镜子
桃花　我看见你时我正走在内心

春天把你送到我小巧的手上
我的手走在你的纹路上
渗透出来的颜色　给我三月的高度
而我在你的体内想象了一个春天
让我忘记一些暗和另一些形态
桃花就要被一场雨拿走　我在雨那边等候

Peach Blossom

Peach blossom, I was in darkness when I saw you
I saw you by the water
I saw you as I was looking in the upside down mirror

Spring sends you to my nimble hands
My palms touch traces of your grains
You color the March beyond exuberance
Inside your body, I quietly incubate
Spring, and I find music where shadows swing
When the rain plucks all your feathers
I'll be there for you
On the other side of the rain

打开星星的光芒

搬运春天的蜜蜂

这是嗡嗡纷飞的阳光
还带有小寒冷的早晨
连我也要搬到一个春天了
在那些花里被采集出一冬的话语
搬运春天的蜜蜂把那些香给了春风
春风又把那些颜色给了谁
我只看到飞掠花影的背影

Unveiling the Star's Light

Spring Carried by the Bees

Sunlight humming in a still chily morning
I carry myself to be with the Spring
Looking for winter's words in flowers
Scent drifts in the wind, bees buzzing
What colors the wind paints now
I see the quivering stripes of the bees

打开星星的光芒

安静的村庄

我能触摸到麦地的呼吸
我能触摸月光漏在梦里的样子
我还能触摸村庄白天遗漏的细节
在一条弯弯的老街上，是一朵槐花

多么静谧的村庄，我听见小草走进高处
夜游的蝙蝠咬住深夜的碎片
一场小风绕着我的窗台徘徊，徘徊
这该是我想一个人时的动静
是我不留神走出去的相思，也有轻轻的声音
似乎怕惊醒一些秘密
多么安静，我几乎触摸到我储存在大槐树上的岁月
那些经年的梦境，就要哗哗落下

A Peacefull Village

I can feel the breaths of the wheat fields
I can touch the faces in their moonlit dreams
I can recount the stories forgotten from the day
On a winding street a stretches locust flower stretches

Such a Peacefull village. I hear grass walking uphill
Bats nibbling tearing night to pieces
Gentle wind lingering on my windowsill
Lingering is what I would do when my heart is longing
When thought escapes the body unannounced
Secrets undisturbed
Tranquility. Time holds still in an old locust tree
And strings of memories fall with a whoosh

早晨的露滴

它跳下来走进泥土里
唱起秋天的歌谣留下土地
它走得很遥远了
直到摸不清它的脚步声
可是,我一个早晨也没走出它的背影
我的脚湿了
我的脚上落满了它的歌词

Unveiling the Star's Light

Morning Dewdrops

They jump into the ground
Autumn songs rise
And disappear from the land
Going, till no footsteps can be found
All morning I walk in their shadows
My feet wet
And covered with damp letters

一地槐花

这是我在春天散失的
多么美好的一篇散文诗
今天,我感到的香靠向村庄
靠向我亲爱的人
这些碎了的月光,碎了的春天
是哪一只鸟的路程,飘过雨季
飘过陈旧的故事,一节墙上的历史
这一地的槐花又不知是谁的睫毛
是否还留有话语,留有对世界的初念

Unveiling the Star's Light

Locust Flowers

A verse that I cherished
I lost it in the spring
Today I smell a scent drifting towards the village
Closer to my beloved
Shredded moonlight and broken spring
What birds are flying through this rainy season
Through old stories, a ruined wall
Locust flowers scattered, like eye lashes
Or perhaps they are epigraphs
From a long-gone past

夜晚升起在唇沿

是的　我还没有说完
露水就来了
我的唇在露水里　感到了积压
我还要说啊　我的话语跑到草尖上
黑慢慢渗进来
夜晚升起在唇沿
我看见了唇吻的真实
我是紧紧贴在那些灯光和窗上的
我的感受也被风带走

Night Rising

Before I finish saying an utterance
Dewdrop descends, moistening my lips
I feel them accumulate
I want to finish but words hide in grass
Darkness seeps through
Night rests on my lips
I see truth in a kiss
As I lean on the light by the window
Thoughts are taken away by the wind

打开星星的光芒

橘子的月亮

今夜的月亮是一枚橘子
是谁悄悄放在天空的盘子里
那么温暖的样子
那么安静
它就在我的唇上
就在我说出另一边的地方

此时,风送走许多事物
剩下模糊的泥土和一座村庄
橘子的月亮被一只手摘走了
它在一朵云的后面
只剩下了我的想象

Tangerine Moon

Tonight's moon is like a tangerine
Sitting on a celestial plate
Warm and Peacefull
Lingering on the other side of my mouth

Now the wind bids adieu to darkness
Opaque soil and village undisturbed
A hand is picking the tangerine behind the clouds
Who is there with my tangerine

打开星星的光芒

我的窗含满星光

满满的溢着　我觉得我久远
我觉得在纯粹的世界里看见一片雪原
我静静地走过　还有干净的空虚也跟着
我觉得我溢着身体里的光　很久远
而此刻 一片叶子划过
我感到了一阵风的真实
并且看见了一幢高大的楼房
还有一声船笛落在我站立的地方

Unveiling the Star's Light

My Window Full with Starlight

So full it is overflowing, and I feel distanced
Inside this innocence there is a snow field
I walk by it, let airiness trail
And I am glowing from afar
A leaf whooshes through
Wind brings back this truthful moment
Aa a giant building lands before me
Ship horn sounding
Through the window nearby me

深夜

我摸到了它的体温
我摸到它的高度
它只是沉默不语地与我对坐
它只是一只眼看着我

我摸到了它的皱纹
我摸到它的深度
它就在我一只手上安静
它在我与天空对话的时候远去

Late at Night

I feel its body temperature and
I can touch its forehead
It sits quietly across from me
Starring at me with only one eye

I feel its wrinkles spreading
And how deep they get
It rests on my hand, undemanding
Then it gets up and leaves
When I was chatting with the sky

第三辑　我看见秋天了

PART 3 I See the Autumn

打开星星的光芒

看见大片的野菊

小小的火焰
是星星移走的光芒
这些让秋天燃烧的野菊
是从果实内心走出来的语言
那么多　似乎取走土地深处的期待
这些低低的匍匐在地的姿势
是谁的眼眸含尽风华
又是谁额头上的凝思
于某个夜晚　悄悄给秋天落叶的思索

这些静静的小小花环
独自占尽一条古老的河流
它们盛开在流动的镜子一端
它们盛开在秋天思考的路途上
它们成片成片地湿

Unveiling the Star's Light

A Great Stretch of Chrysanthemum Field

Sparkling little flames
Lights from the stars
Wild chrysanthemums set autumn on crimson fire
Words walk out of harvests
With anxiety and hope
Above the ground, crawling blossoms
Like thoughts on my mind
Soon to pass, to falling leaves

Peacefull garlands afloat on ageless river
They bloom on the edges of a traveling mirror
Along a road heavy with footprints
Blotches of damp memories remain

打开星星的光芒

露滴

我看见了透亮的露滴
在草上摇晃
我看见露滴在秋天的肩头
是另一种成熟的果实
这些晶莹的宝贝
在谁的手掌上转动
在谁的眼角溢着温存
那么亲切

露滴　你要悄悄走下阳光的梯子
你要把身体埋在叶落的地方
你要把短暂的生命给予
哪怕是瞬间被一只鹰翅掠过
哪怕你只留下颤动

Dewdrops

I see translucent dewdrops
Swinging on grass tips
I see dewdrops spreading out on fall's shoulder
And ripening fruits
Crystal genies, pirouetting on a palm
Corners of my eyes soft with admiration

Dewdrops stepping down sun's ladder
Hiding underneath fallen leaves
Now I ponder on mortality and effort
I see a bird, let it be an eagle
Let its wings brush over you
With a blow, or a tremble

打开星星的光芒

我看见秋天了

秋天在一枚果实上走
把天空说成一首诗
那些飞雁背起一处水域,一座山
一座村庄的故事
被一场雨静静地湿透
还有寻找另一个我的蝴蝶
她很累了,在草尖上与一个黄昏融合

我看见秋天了
秋天在云的意象上翻卷出一次重生
秋天在我咬破的苹果上
另一些累累地挂着　压弯了我的思路

I See the Autumn

Fall is treading on the face of a fruit
Talking poetry to the sky
Geese carry a river and mountain on their backs
Stories of a village silently soaking in the rain
Where are the butterflies, the one I missed
Tired and perhaps resting on twilight's branch

I see the autumn
I see clouds rolling and reincarnating
Autumn sits on an apple that I took a bite of
And the season's apples hang heavy on the trees
They bend me and the branches

打开星星的光芒

秋天的爱情

秋天的爱情是深夜的虫鸣
一枚干净的叶子与天空
那种神秘悄悄被风卷起
太多时候,秋天走在果实的背面
有紫色的背影
一片云触到了雨水的沉静
就像一汪水倒映出季节的过程
有谁独自低吟,夜深深

秋天的爱情是夜莺歌唱
是月光的花瓣
花瓣编制的篮子
要装下什么,装下什么
这个时候,不想离别

Autumn Love

Autumn love is a bug's song on dark nights
A lucid leaf facing the tall sky
Mysterious being unfolding in the wind
And behind the wheels, harvests
A purple back gleaming
Only the clouds know the stillness before the rain
Iike a puddle of soft water displaying the season
Who is humming at night
Lonesome and content?

Autumn love, sweet nightingale singing
Petals of the moon with ripe scent
Baskets woven with petals, such fragrant being
Too painful to leave

打开星星的光芒

搬运秋天的蚂蚁

它们忙碌在树上
不知在哪棵树上忙碌
黑色的精灵,一天天瘦下来
它们要搬运一个可储存的天空
要搬运一个风中的记忆
它们赶着自己黑色的血
把秋天搬进身体

这些缄默的黑色使者
它们要传递一封什么样的书信
在脊背上,我感到了沉重
感到它们把整个秋天都当作一种歌唱

Unveiling the Star's Light

Ants Carrying the Fall

Busy inside, invisible trees
Dark spirits, thinner and thinner like autumn twigs
Shuffle the sky above, piece by piece
And store memories for safekeeping
Teeny blood cells drive unceasingly
Soon autumn will be moved to their colonies

Silent little messengers with secret correspondence
I feel their heavy loads
And hear their song
In dotted long lines
A quiet chorus for the season

打开星星的光芒

秋菊

这些小小洁玉之身
守候一枚又一枚果实的回望
她们舞蹈在风中
我望见她们爬山的背影
涉水时小心翼翼地低垂
我望见她们在雨中一次走失又回来
秋菊　洗清河流的妹子
今天　阳光朗照　聆听远方的妹子
我仿佛感到上升的火焰　正燃烧秋天
那些白色火焰　将映照一场大雪
那些大雪是秋菊匍匐在地的梦境

Autumn Chrysanthemum

Lucid and chaste
Dutifully guard the season's harvest
They waltz in the wind
And swing towards the mountains
They tread through waters, eyes fixed and knees bent
They fall and rise in wheels of the season
Autumn fairies bring me sunny days
Songs of flames rising above fecund land
White hot flames, emblematic of snow storms
And snow
Will soon arrive with a reverence

打开星星的光芒

秋水

你深入水果
我食果而思
你身上的星星都是雨滴
你印证的树木都有弯曲　宿鸟沉默
我看见你被山记录的事件被一朵花偷走
花沉重　花在你身上
秋水　我看见你一步步退到石头内部
你遗留的湿地上　天空多了一些额纹

Autumn Water

You are a well inside a fruit
I savor your juice
Raindrops fall like shooting stars
So precious they are your flesh and bones
Trees carry you to the tallest branch, birds nest still
Mountainside gulches store your every visit
Quenching flowers with heavy petals
Autumn water, this time you are lowering your brims
Returning home to cracked stones
Leaving behind a damp patch
And in the sky a few more wrinkles

打开星星的光芒

一叶秋风

它将被一枚果实记住
或者被一群雁鸣背起
它将是一片叶子的样子
在飘的时候生动了秋色

它将会是永远的记忆　在泥土的怀里
有时候我会不经意地触动了它的安静
就在我几乎被秋天占有的时候
一叶秋风　就做了我内心的旗帜

Autumn Breeze

You are to be remembered by a fruit
Or carried under a flock of geese
Autumn breeze, you gather into the shape of a leaf
Stirring up fall brilliance

You are a permanent memory inside the soil
Where I find peace in solitude
A leaf I turn for redemption
Autumn breeze raises a flag inside the soul

打开星星的光芒

秋风吹进我内心

这丰盈着粮食　果实的秋风
从叶子上跳下来
从一场雨的韵律里跳下来
从灿烂的早晨　摘下一朵云后跳下来
在我措手不及之时　秋风
我感到了你倒出来的田野香

我多愿你不住地吹起
多愿在我的衣角掀起天空的时候
让你丰厚的主题替我带上永久的愿望
此时　我站在你的中心
看见鸟起伏在田野　看见大片的粮地生动
此时　多愿吹进我内心的风　堆起过冬的种子

Autumn Wind Blowing into My Heart

Autumn wind in the fields, plump and fruitful
Jumping off the leaves, off from the rain
On morning's tiptop, you swell
From behind a cloud catch me in surprise
And I inhale eagerly
Ripe fragrance pouring where you go

How I wish you'd never stop, lifting me up
As you take me by the corners of my shirt
Like birds over the fields, I am amongst you
Such colors and richness beneath
And I dive for them and gather seeds for my winter

打开星星的光芒

几片卷曲的落叶

这是从夜晚的风暴中走下来的
它们抱着各自的姿势
似乎是谁丢弃的目光
今天　在早晨就击中我

而我就在它们中间
保留着自己的神情
一场风暴没给我带来什么
我只是看到那些脆弱者　一地呻吟

Unveiling the Star's Light

A Few Curled Leaves

They came from last night's storm
Holding their last shapes
Tired eyes hitting me right in this morning

So I stay with them
Maintaining my own shape like a leaf
The storm is for me nothing
But those weak and brittle, now still quivering

打开星星的光芒

秋天的抒情

秋天　说来就来了
我也隐现在一场雨的背后
先看见果实、粮食点燃的村庄
草背起了天空　河流沿岸走过

我看见成群的鸟像另一些树叶
它们挤进风的姿态让秋天更深沉
在每个深夜都会听见辽阔的虫鸣
我都会在虫鸣拥挤的地方
惦记一片悄悄走来的叶子
我都会在露水打湿的路上
听取关于秋天的生动

秋天　来得悄然啊
有的生命还未转身就被挫伤
今天又多了一地风扫的痕迹
然而还有更多的生命
坚持在暴雨袭击的傍晚
没有期待　更多的是燃烧

看见吗　那些盛开的秋菊
依然挣出草根沸腾着土地
看见吗　还有更多雨后新生的草　又来
似乎又一种希望让天空的云朵一次次运载
而秋天也终会成熟的
是在种子的梦里　在一朵花走过的地方
而秋天终会走回泥土
在大地的光环里　在一场雪灿烂的光环里

打开星星的光芒

A Love Song for the Fall

Fall descends in a timely fashion
Calling me to emerge from a shadow after the rain
Harvest season, crops light up villages
Grass stakes the sky's tent
Rivers softly tread and glow

I see flocks of birds flying like leaves
How they expand inside the wind
Offer the season solid existence
Every night I hear insects singing in chorus
And I join the crowd, feeling exuberance like a leaf
I walk like tall grass on the country road
Quenching thirst with the morning dew

Such tranquil descending
Unprepared lives injured, by no intent
A few mornings torn by storms
Still the brave determined

Unveiling the Star's Light

Awaiting the season's last torch

Chrysanthemums are in full bloom
Springing out of turbulent burning
Like grass returning after each rain
Patches of clouds forever restore
Fall matures as seeds dream of sprouting
And flowers return to soil
Grand homecoming now awaits
The brilliant glow of a warm snow

打开星星的光芒

走进秋天的腹地

秋天　天空也在你的中央
厚重成饱满的种子
在一阵阵饱酌果实的风里
深情成一片叶子

秋天　我正在诵读一座粮田
我占据在一块天空的蓝里
把风想象成火
通过一只蝴蝶想象
通过一朵野菊梦见的梦想象
在一场风雨抵达之前
我收拾起那些遍野的虫鸣
守候在一棵树的根部
遇见流水怎样搬运这一个季节的重

Unveiling the Star's Light

Walking on Autumn's Hinterland

Autumn, sky is amidst you
Thickening into plump seeds
Wind carries scent of harvests
Leaves deep in colors of affection

I'm citing a poem about the fields
About taking a corner in the sky's blue
Imagine wind catching flames
And the burnt, morphing into butterflies
And chrysanthemums
Now I quietly round up the bugs before the storms
Crouching by a tree and we watch patiently
Water shifts between seasons

第四辑　春天的声音

PART 4 Sound of the Spring

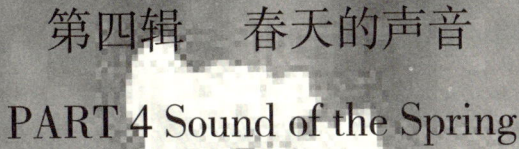

打开星星的光芒

一片叶子

一片叶子划过黄昏
亲切的叶子　我看见了你上面的先前
我生锈的城市　街道　母亲的手以及炊烟
都卷曲成风的样子　而我叶子的目光
还在我转身之时停留过纪念
现在　眼前的叶子落下来
正落在我三十岁的年轮
我的夜晚　早晨　我的责任使叶子持重
我感到了疼痛　如手的叶子与你融合
我看见了你的飘　是我所有的感动

A Leaf

A leaf streaks across dusk, carrying its
Rusty city, the streets
Mother's hand and smoke from the chimney
All in the wind
I turn my back and pause to commemorate
Eyes on the falling leaves
Down to my 30 years old growth ring
Mundane mornings, evenings, and duties
Extra weight on your wings, you keep flying
And now your falling is causing me pain
I reach out my hand towards you
Catching you in midair, with gratitude

打开星星的光芒

我以一朵花的姿势开放

我只选择花的姿势
永远不被淋湿或者风中夭折
我保持花的美　花占据了我整个身体
多少年一直这样
我沉静如夜晚　我的花瓣点缀星星的愿望
并且不被烧毁
很多时候　我都保持这样
城市做了我的花骨　生活做了我的颜色

Unveiling the Star's Light

Blooming Like a Flower

I only choose to be the essence of a flower
Not to be rained on or blown off by the wind
I choose to maintain beauty inside this body
And let that be always
Calm in dark nights, still blooming
Petals glinting from the stars
And stars glow but will not burn
Forever genuine and curious with my city
Strong for the flower's backbones
And all days in rainbow colors

打开星星的光芒

有一种飞都有蝴蝶的内心

这是我相挽春天想到的
临水的草　花的姿态　解开储存远方纽扣的叶子
高飞的鸟　行走的云　打开河水想象的风
还有涨溢在深夜的梦　一个早晨和一个黄昏
它们都有蝴蝶的心境
那种美像一个少女手提陶罐去阳光里汲水
是啊　有一种飞是看不见的
内心的蝴蝶早已占尽春天的细节
这时候黑暗也是温暖的　生命中的光明替代一种勇气
它们在春天巨大的影子里拿出最初的真诚

Unveiling the Star's Light

A Butterfly's Soul

This is my encounter with the spring
Weeds by the water, vibrant flowers
Leaves unbuttoning distant mysteries
Birds flying high in clouds' drift
Winds unleashing river's desires
Rising midnight dreams
Dawn and dusk with gentle souls
Beauty is this girl with an urn
Carrying water from the sunlit creek
And the souls are flying
Spreading spring on butterfly's wings
Such a time when darkness has warmth
And courage lights up deep tunnels
Utter truthfulness I only see
Rising above spring's giant shadow

打开星星的光芒

我是岛上的一只蝴蝶

我忽略水那边的楼群　窗户和街道
我侧过城市的颜色与一场雨无助地述说
在接近潮语与光的纯粹里
我忘记古老的忧伤和眼前的迷茫
我是岛上的一只蝴蝶　是你诗歌的文字
在夜晚里读你神情的疏放
读你黑夜里点播的星光以及你慢下来的脚步
我逢遇你目光的内涵　你露水的眼
我逢遇你供奉泥土的意义　你蔓延的草尖
我在风里翩然　在你发上吟唱
寄存一万年前的爱情
把我轻的骨骼给你　给你岛上每一块岩石

Unveiling the Star's Light

A Butterfly on an Island

I ignore the tall buildings, windows and streets
On the other side of the water
I turn sideways to view the city's profile
Converse with the rain
Approach tides and lights in their purest forms
Letting go tiresome melancholy and confusion
An island butterfly spreading genuine words
Console darkness, sow seeds deep
Slow down to find sweetness
In grass, flowers, water and air
Now I land on your hair, leaving you with this
Love song that's been sung for ten thousand years
And at last, I shall hang up my light bones
On the face of a cliff by the sea

打开星星的光芒

鸥鸟

鸥鸟似乎是走远的大海浪尖
一只落在水上　一只高盘　一只如箭
翻飞出阳光重生的词语
又似乎我眉间苏醒的文字在写着什么
这些鸥鸟是在获取一方土地上的意义
一座城市的生动也被烘托到窗上
还有延伸在我心土的道路
像极了鸥鸟的形象

Gulls

Clipping the tips of waves
Landing on water, rising up and soaring like a spear
Towards sunlight
Reaching for forgotten words
You wake me up with lines between my brows
Taking my quest under your wings
You light up the city on my windowsill
Now the dusty road transforms, its shape
A gull
And a runway with you taking off

我听见了什么

那是一个词语复活的夜晚
没有打招呼就把一河的水放出来
那是一朵花去年的睡眠
没有解释就把原野拢起来
那是一滴水从冰尖上划出的小路
没有说什么就铺成了一封信笺

我都听见了
只是悄悄走开
只是不去打搅那些渗进的新声
我知道　春要挤破一冬的镜子了

Unveiling the Star's Light

I Hear

That was a night's murmurs when dead words resurrected
Water running free from the river, unafraid
That was the voice of an old dream in a flower's sleep
Circulating the desert, unrestrained
And that was a road being carved out
By the tip of an iceberg
Now laying flat like a clean piece of paper

I hear all of them
And I slowly walk away
Not to disturb new sounds coming
And I know as I am waiting
Spring is ready
Soon to break free and shatter winter's mirror

打开星星的光芒

开放

谁听见天空开放的声音
谁听见蓝色开放的声音
云思考的一个冬季　开始疏松了额纹
就在风的指尖　点缀世界
开放　大地上挤满了新的眼神
大地上的三月是最高处的翅膀
此起彼伏
此时　我也解开衣扣　装满道路

Unveiling the Star's Light

In Full Bloom

Do you hear the sky cracking?
And the blooming blue
Clouds pondering on winter, relaxing their grips
Fingers of the wind tidying up decorations
Blooming is everywhere, everything
The land is packed with new eyes blinking
March rides on its highest wings
Surging through
And now I unbutton my shirt
And roll up the road's sleeves

打开星星的光芒

溪边的一棵小草

水不动声色地流着
小鱼在水里多幸福
我看着时就照见了自己
我还顶着露珠　低着头

水流逝了我的心事
小鱼含着我的秘密
我想着时风又来说着什么
我的内心越来越翠绿

Grass by a Creek

Water quietly flowing
Content fish
I see in my reflection
Dewdrops on my head as I stoop

The creek clears up my thinking
Fish swarms with my secrets
Now the wind starts to say something
I blush, and turn even more green

打开星星的光芒

春风拂过来

春风拂过来　真痒
就像心尖的刺秘密地扎我
就像蚂蚁咬住我昨夜的不眠
我的目光也漏了　兜不住想

轻柔的春风摇着新的叶子
摇着远处的风景
多像我在你名字一边的姿势
多像我眼角的一滴泪水　也浸着春天
可是我抵不住风的呼唤
就像一朵花悄悄开着

Spring Breeze

Spring puffs and tickles
Poking like an invisible thorn
Ants crawl in my insomnia
And secrets leaking out in the morning gaze

Spring breeze rocks new leaves
Landscape swinging in the distance
Such as how I lay by your name
A soft tear in the eye's corner
All suited for the wakening season
Only I can't resist the call of the breeze
And yearn to rise quietly and bloom

打开星星的光芒

春晚如花

夕阳摇着树梢上的天空
金子的土地上　一条江流过我和村庄
群鸟翻找出一个遥远
古老的歌谣被春风唱颂

此时　我走在它巨大的花瓣上
像一片云　一角轻轻卷起
此时　我有了第一颗星子的目光
我看着那光　悄悄戴在手指上

Unveiling the Star's Light

Spring Night Blossom

Sunset stirs up the sky on the tips of the tree
Over the golden field, a river through my village
A flock of birds digging a distant past
An old tune echoes in the spring breeze

Now I walk on a giant flower petal
Like a cloud rolling a soft sleeve
My eyes catch light of the first star
Discreetly, I place it on my ring finger

打开星星的光芒

小竹林

这么安静
竹叶上的天空让我安静下来
早晨　黄昏是纯粹的
我守着虫鸣和一截墙
守着叶子走远又回来
然后我看见我三十岁的窗户
一天　我的梦淌出来
就浸泡了一块手上的石子
一天　我发现身后的城市也是石子

Little Bamboo Forest

Tranquility
Sky above the bamboo, celestial gleam
Dawn and dusk in their purest forms
I guard them, and guard the sound of bugs
Leaning on a section of wall ruins
I stay with the leaves as they depart and return
And I see through a window of thirty years
One day a dream climbed over the sill
A gem landed on my palm, softened by heat
And then I found the city behind me
A giant stone of granite

打开星星的光芒

夜

我听见声音藏进深处
另一些声音走出来
我如蹚起一汪的水　裤脚湿着
我在走向谁
夜　我看着星星的走向
我看着它们背上的光
我跟着原野和一朵花的心境
我慢慢剩下半个身子

Night

I hear sound hiding in a deep place
Different sounds overlap
I wade across a pool of water
The bottom of my trousers wet
Who am I walking towards?
Night, I see stars' movement, glinting
I follow the desert and the scent of a blossom
Now slowly only half a body left
Half conscious

打开星星的光芒

一抹夕阳

这是一条路冷静下来的颜色
靠近水声
一边擦着天空的玻璃
一边看着土地
此时　夕阳还在我指尖
像一只鸟　一只飞进星星里的鸟
我看见它的背影　火一样
它走进一片黑夜

Unveiling the Star's Light

Sunset

This is the color of a road cooling down
Closer to the sound of water
Clouds brushing and wiping while looking down
Now the rays descend on my fingertips
A bird ascends towards the stars
And I see its shadow, like a fire ball
Blazing through darkness

打开星星的光芒

月亮的花瓣

我在月亮的花瓣上
我想着时别人看见是一滴露
风拂过来　我抖了一下身子
拾起掉落的神
月亮的花瓣盛开夜的秘密
我在想着一座村庄的样子
那座村庄也在花瓣上
我不知道它在想什么
风不住地摇着花瓣
万万年了　不住地凋谢　盛开

Unveiling the Star's Light

Petals of the Moon

I sit on a petal of the moon
A drop of dew moistens the look
Wind gives me a gentle shake and I bend over
What was lost there, my composure
Moon petals reveal the night's secrets
A village looms so vividly in my eyes
My village is sitting on a petal too
What's she thinking? I don't know
I only know petals quiver in the wind
For a million years
Wind will keep on coming and going
And petals of the moon will always
Wither and bloom

下部

第一辑 雨季之外

PART 1 After the Monsoon

打开星星的光芒

一个梦

你看不透沙滩上无数脚印
也许已经走出很远
这些沧桑一万年后进入一棵树
淡淡月光下　你的徘徊是大海的回声
是一棵树在泥水里的盘根
这是你突然闯进的境遇
树上结满无数眼睛　空灵的眼睛
在风中颤动
你看见失眠与忧伤　激动与绽放
这些冥冥中的花朵　在海岸持久
一万年的姿态细数一万次事件
偶然与必然
这些风流就是金子的沙粒
你走过时有多少辗转
飞鸟与鱼雁侧身掠过　闪过的影子
在大海与树木　光明与黑暗的切入
有谁怀揣最大的恩赐
而时间在放牧的海水之上

Unveiling the Star's Light

时间在树木的枝柯与枝柯之间回旋
你一个梦中清醒的人
指尖轻弹的古老琵琶
是梦中移动的另一个你
星子是眼睛　沙滩是背影
这么些年　你一直做同样的梦
你驻足于大海与树木的外延
驻足于流逝与存在的荒芜
还有谁能在沉迷中摇醒
这不是迷失，你的内心是一片浮叶
你看见那些远去的手臂　无数双手臂
那些背影　留下刻痕的背影
或许是春天之华　秋季之实
那些人为的阶梯　历史的裂痕哦
生命之光　不是文字的厚度

打开星星的光芒

A Dream

You can't follow those footprints on the beach
Countless, extending a long way
A tree holds ten thousand years of life
Under the pale moonlight, your swing echoes ocean waves
Like a tree spreading roots in muddy water
Your swiftly encounter
Those eyes in the tree, eyes of souls
Shivering in the wind
You see insomnia and melancholy
Thrill and blossoms
Flowers glinting by the shore, been there for a long time
Ten-thousand times correlate ten-thousand occurrences
Accidental or inevitable
Specks in the golden sand brushed by wind
How much grinding you went through
Birds and geese tipping their wings, shadows flashing by
Between the ocean and woods, light and darkness mingle
Who holds more gratitude

Unveiling the Star's Light

Time flies over the ocean, a prairie of water
Circulating the trees, in thick branches
You are totally conscious in your dreams
Plucking the strings of an ancient lute
That is another you lost in dreams
Stars are your eyes, the beach holds your back
This is a reoccurring dream for many years
You dwell on the outskirts of the ocean and trees
Dwelling in the wasteland of passage and existence
Who can awaken you in such indulgence
You are not lost, simply holding onto a floating leaf
You see arms moving away from you, countless arms
Those faces turning their back on you, back with deep carvings
This may be part of spring's rise and autumn harvest
Steps laid by man, and cracks in history
Light of life, beyond words

打开星星的光芒

燃烧的花瓣

雨水退到季节之外
遍布的预言　谁是怀疑者
翻卷的云渐渐隐去
天空在燃烧
星光　这巨大的花瓣照见了什么
树木的仰望固执而坚定
大海在燃烧
它的花瓣是潮汐　一次次地涌动遥远
谁的影子在海面上沉浮？
鹰收起它的翅膀止于平静
雨水退到季节之外
石头在燃烧　它神秘、缄默
只有敲打　厚重的历史一闪而过
土地也在燃烧
它的燃烧是早晨与夜晚的章节
树木卷起土地的颜色
就像一场盛大的表演
现在　你站在边缘地带

承受一次洗礼
你看见勤劳的人民在劳作
汗水湿过泥土
这些蝴蝶的款款之飞
让世界在你的外部像一个黑点
这个巨大背景复杂而矛盾
你只是一次生命的忽略或未来的替代者

打开星星的光芒

Flaming Petals

Rain backs away from the season
Widespread forecasts, arising skepticism
Whirling clouds disappear
Sky is burning
Starlight, what the gigantic petal is to unveil
Gaze of trees, steadfast and determined
The sea is on fire
Tides grow ocean's petals, rushing to reach afar
Time and time again, floating shadows belonging to whom
Seagulls unfold their wings in silence

Rain backs away from the season
Stone burns in mystery and silence
Chipping away thick history
Land catches fire too
Flaming dust and dawn, chapters of time
Trees lift the color of the earth
Raising the curtain on a stupendous performance

Unveiling the Star's Light

Now you stand near the edge, being baptized
You witness hard-working people
Sweatier than the wet soil
Butterflies showing their elegance
Your outside world looks like a giant speck
Against a huge backdrop of complexity and contradiction
You are just a being, life's neglect
Or a substitute in the future

风中的菊花

这是九月　我的身体靠近一枚菊花
衣袂飘起时　我在花瓣上静思风尘
这是我与它潜在的联系
菊花的香溢满我的手掌
它与我都在风中
在静默的时候我们相互抑制
彼此保持一种秋天
而菊花会早夭的　会剩下我
会剩下我在秋香里怀恋瘦下来的思绪

Unveiling the Star's Light

Chrysanthemum in the Wind

This is September, I stand close to a chrysanthemum
My cloth is billowing as I'm meditating on a flower petal
The scent of chrysanthemum fills the palm of my hand
We are both submerged in the wind restraining one another in silence
Maintaining the composure of the fall
While this flower will die young, I shall remain
Feeling melancholy with withering thoughts
Floating in the subtle scent

打开星星的光芒

一株草黄了

这些黄是它体内的金子
金子的颜色在风中
而我感到是一次远行的姿态
它周身的时间不住地散发
我发现时在玩弄自己的手指
也没有感觉到时间的爬行走进体内
或许那株草正发现我　它也正玩弄手指
秋天了　一株草替我思考了许多泥泞

A Withered Grass

Such yellow is the gold inside your body
The gold shines in the wind
Yet I sense readiness for a long journey
Time is evaporating inside you
I found myself playing with my fingers as I was watching you
Unaware of the time entering and leaving
Perhaps you too were playing with your fingers
After all it's the fall season
The grass is heaped with enlightenment
Helping me through the mud

打开星星的光芒

叶子的自语

雨水正慢慢远去
你的面容开始憔悴
你弯成一座桥的样子
有无名的风悄悄走过
一只鸟还在你身上翻找什么
这个时候　黑夜在你体内膨胀
你已是土地的颜色了
土地深处有沉睡的水域
那些匍匐在地的藤蔓
如隐藏的牙齿紧紧咬住一片片水域
你看到那些埋藏的火山
看到火山深处沉默的岩浆
而这些沉静的事物似乎是亿万年前的场景
此时　一朵花飘落在你的桥上
如同一尾失血的羽毛

A Leaf's Soliloquy

The rain is receding
Your face sallow
You bend into the shape of a bridge
Unnamed wind quietly blows over you
A bird is fumbling through your branches for something
And now darkness is expanding inside you
You turn into the color of soil
Underneath the soil is water asleep
Vines crawling
like invisible teeth biting onto bank of water
You see a volcano buried deep
Lava waiting to ignite in silence
And these were scenes from millions of years ago
Now a flower lands on your bridge
Like a bloodless feather

岸上的影子

这是雨季之岸
雨水在内心丢失
现在　你走过一座城市
城市在变小
你遇见很多人　很多人在奔跑
你遇见橱窗、高速路　还有更高的楼
在你遇见时　它们是城市的影子
城市是岸的影子
你走过时　看见影子很薄　像一张纸

Unveiling the Star's Light

Shadows over the River Bank

On the edge of the monsoon
Rain escaped your mind
Now you walk by a city
The city is shrinking
You see many people running
Shop windows, highways, and tall buildings
Shadows of your city
And the city casts a shadow by the bank
You walk by, a hollow and thin piece of paper

打开星星的光芒

失踪

许多人失踪了　失踪在一堵墙里
经年的墙裂出了缝隙
一些人的影子经常在夜里出现
而土地上的树木依然疯长
海水的巨大花环下，还有忧虑的人走过
古老的笛音，悠长于枫叶的燃烧
谁是失踪的人
群鸟的翅膀涌起春天之潮
群山的高度在不动声色地凝视
谁是失踪的人
我翻找在梦里，我拨开流水
荒域或久已生锈的琴音
被我怀念的古战场上的风
被我占据心灵无法挣脱的大漠孤烟
又被我一次次递进内心的史诗
我总矗立于宁静的黄昏及街市
在一块巨大广告牌下面　沉思

Lost

Many are missing, vanishing into the walls

Aged walls with veins

Shadowy figures converge at night

Trees undergoing growth spurts

Under the massive garland of the ocean

Melancholic beings pass through

Sounds of ancient flutes, outlasting the burns of the maple leaves

Who is missing

Bird wings lift waves of spring

Mountain tops gaze into the distance

What is missing?

I search through my dreams, diving in streams

Sound of music, rusting away

And deserted land

Rekindling ancient battle fields ---

I recall them

A lonesome smoky desert fills my soul

Surrendering epic lines from the heart

I stand on the street in the twilight zone of the city

Lost, under a giant billboard

打开星星的光芒

钥匙

我的钥匙丢了
我的脚下都是落叶
都有钥匙的形状
我的翻找让一本书模糊
我的钥匙丢了
河水无声流过,石头坚持
我在大树下孤立成一个象征
就像一只空置的手掌
风呼呼而过
好久了,我在寻找那把真正的钥匙
我看见花朵收藏的早晨
热烈的夏季;雪花写意的天空
好久了,我一直敲打一座桥
我看见桥上的人,桥上看人的人
雨中戴草帽的人　醉中的人
赤裸奔跑的画也在一座桥上展示
这时,我会打开一张白纸
什么也不说,然后任灯光点燃
如同静默时打开一条道路

Keys

I lost my keys
Underneath my feet are fallen leaves
Shaped like keys
My book turned blurry as I flipped it through
For the lost keys
Rivers run through in silence; stones remain still
My lone figure under a tree becomes a symbol
Iike an empty palm of a hand
Wind whistling by
I am searching for the truth
I see the morning hiding blossoms
Passionate summer; snowflakes painting the impressionistic sky
It's been a long while, I knock on a bridge
I see people on the bridge, people watching other people
Men wearing straw hats in the rain
Drunk men running naked
Now I lay out a piece of blank paper
Wordless, I let the candle burn, as if to
Give light to a quiet path

打开星星的光芒

秋风早晨

我走在叶子的飘里
我走在燃烧的缝隙里
我静静地走过秋天早晨
我说我走过时留下一幅油画
而我两手空空
我正等待着提起那个天空的篮子

Morning Wind in the Fall

I hover above the drifting leaves
I walk on the cracks of burnt ruins
I stroll through this autumn morning
leaving behind an oil painting
And my hands are free, ready to
Lift up the basket
Beholding the sky

打开星星的光芒

中秋月

我看见了白　亿万年的白
这是谁的骨子的光
让野地沉静得泛着花语
此时　我似乎触摸到月光里的流水
或者一个人梦见的姿势
此时　我在秋天的中央　在月光
在白的一枚羽毛上充当了另一只鸟
今夜　我一直保持飞的样子
在光华里腾起秋天的意义
可飞跃不出自己
而月光照见了一种力量

Unveiling the Star's Light

Mid-autumn Moon

I see whiteness in the pale moon, distilled through a billion years
Whose pallid bone light
Calming the wilderness, floral yield
I can feel the flowing water in the spread of the moon
Perhaps in someone's dream
Now this is the middle of fall, the center of the moon
On the tip of a white feather sits a bird
Tonight I am ready, holding a flying position
Lifting up this high season with its offerings
Though I shall not rise above myself
The moon awaits to exert its force

打开星星的光芒

树梢上的月亮

这是我看到的最干净的月亮
在九月的深夜　我没有怀疑其他事物的参与
至少我感到自己有些不合时宜
我怕着一点思绪就会搅乱这份宁静
这份被世界空出来的光亮
零点了　我左右为难
我在虫鸣不辍的草地里晾晒着昨天的身体
只想保持这干净的气氛
只想把自己浸泡在月光里
不为什么　不为什么　风终会悄悄把我捆走

Unveiling the Star's Light

Moon Clipping the Tree

This moon is in its utter perfection, its purest
Deep September night with no interference
None that I feel suitable to take part of
Fearful that the slightest distraction would disrupt the peace
This brightness emptied out by the world
Ambivalent midnight
I am bathing in the lawn, humming a bug's song
No other intent but to keep this pureness
Soaking in the moonlight
And wind will come by and hush me away

打开星星的光芒

秋雁

这是一行诗句
我看见有一种力量的穿行
在楼群上空　在夜沉下来的时候
我看见远走的文字　体现着什么
大地在凝望　星星亮起了眼睛
秋雁　一声声鸣唱辽阔
谁能挽住这些辽阔的声音
谁就读懂了秋天的意义
此时　这一行诗句隐藏在远处的灯光里
此时　我正弯腰拾着什么

Unveiling the Star's Light

Autumn Geese

It is a line of poetry
I see a subtle force running though
Above the buildings when night falls
I see words walking in the distance, with reflections
The earth is gazing, stars opening their eyes
Autumn geese, bellowing in vastness
Those who harvest such grand voice are sages of the season
A line of poetry shines in the distance
And I see it as I bend over
Gathering

打开星星的光芒

我坐下来,秋天高高在上

我坐在几枚落叶祭奠的黄昏
成熟的果实要留下光
成熟的声音要压弯最高的枝头
还有一片片云建筑的天宇
都在沉静如水的土地上刻下弧线
这是高高在上的秋天
近旁一卷雨书,一只蚂蚁穿过
近旁一条河流正载走一个早晨
近旁,还有一片空旷正等待装扮什么

我静谧地坐着
看着事物离开季节的背影
看着一次与我相挽的远方,几种神秘几种神态
我会把内心掏出来
希望交给诵读秋风的枫叶
交给占居草地上的野菊
希望它们也举起我,像谁家的风筝看尽风华
此时,我只有交出唯一的静穆
 在粮食喂养的土地上

在我们喂养的土地上
在城市,村庄装满你最后思考的路上
摘不下这一颗最亮的星星

我坐下来,秋天高高在上
风呼呼喊出又一种征途
我感到那些隐秘的光环别在万家
那些让我高仰的过程闪现在果实的沉静里
那些让我说不出的,没有名分的事物
还在我思绪中生发

打开星星的光芒

Under the High Autumn Sky

I sit in twilight with fallen leaves
Mature fruits straining to hold light inside
Sound of ripening bends tall branches
Skyscrapers propped up by clouds
Shadows draw curvy lines
On the ground calm as the back of hands
Such high autumn sky
Nearby rain, an ant walking through
Nearby a river, carrying away the day
Nearby, an empty space awaits embellishments

I sit here quietly, watching the season's departure
A faraway place where I held hands once
Secret places and bygones
I shall let out my heart and let it sing
For the maple leaves singing Psalms of the season
For the chrysanthemums dancing in the fields
They shall raise me up like a kite
And at last I hand over my solitude

To the soil that is fed by us and feeds us
To the city and the country that occupy the minds
leaving behind one brightest lone star

Under the high sky of fall I sit
Whispering wind beckons me to a new journey
Gleaming garlands discreetly hung on doors
How I admire the calmness of the harvest
And many unnamed things, indescribable
Looming large inside me

打开星星的光芒

一只鸟飞出静夜

我看见时那些窗上的亮都走了
只有我与一江的水默语
这只鸟是飞出来了
像一片叶子
鸟啊　你偷走了谁的梦　这么匆匆
此时鸟是幸福的　连影子都没有漏掉
此时我就占据在静寂的地方
看着看着　我也张开了臂膀

Unveiling the Star's Light

A Bird Flies Away on a Tranquil Night

Light in the window darkens when I see it
Leaving me and a river facing silence
This bird escaped
Iike a leaf blown away
Oh bird, did you snatch up a dream, hurriedly
The bird looks auspicious, having not missed a beat
Now I'm taking a place of tranquility, watching
And slowly opening up my wings

打开星星的光芒

一只翅膀飞过泥泞

一只翅膀　深入夜晚的翅膀
它的持重有无数雨点的扩张
它的飞有河流的姿态
有岩石的姿态　有叶片的姿态
这些被词语消解
这些在弯曲的岸上延伸
某一时辰　你也是一只翅膀
持重的翅膀
重现的泥泞在门之外　窗之外

第一辑　雨季之外

A Wing Flying Over a Muddy Field

A lone wing entering the dark night
Soaked in rain, tipping the balance
It has the shape of a river's course
And the shape of a rock's face, of a leaf
Beyond words
It lends a symbol on the curvy bank
As you turn into a wing, a weight bearing wing
The reoccurring mud is outside your door
And your window

打开星星的光芒

我也是一枚种子

我会悄悄把走过来的夜埋进泥土
我会沉静下来　在一场雨后清洗身子
我还会依在一块石头旁　说着故事
就这样　看着过往的时间把冬天搬过来
我必定是一枚种子了
沉淀在一个脚印里
而我怀揣的季节还要归还
现在我的样子只是暂且把生命积攒

Unveiling the Star's Light

A Seed

Discreetly I bury the nights that I walked by
I shall remain my composure, cleansing myself after the rain
I shall also lean on a rock, and tell a story
Just like that, I watch time moving winter towards me
I must be a seed
Sediment under a footprint
Yet this season when I grew must return
And I'm accumulating life, one season at a time

打开星星的光芒

小路上的脚印

重叠了的空间　任风吹过
小路默然　小路上的脚印分散
像一条很旧的绳结
曾收留过鸟鸣　一个人的背影
或一个季节的淡定
某一天　你会重新陷入
像雨水带来重生
你将把远方还给雨点
某一天　你还会温暖地走过
就像一场久违的安静
你有蝴蝶的印象

Unveiling the Star's Light

Footprints on a Trail

Space folds and overlaps as the wind blows
The quiet trail, footprints scattered
Like an old rope twisted with knots
Bird's chirping, back of a lone man
Unconcerned about the season
Yet some days you fall hard for it all over again
Like rain bringing life for reincarnation
You send the rain a faraway place
Someday, you will walk through the warmth again
Feeling nostalgically Peacefull
And recall impression of butterflies

且行且远

你什么时候忘记路已不是路
都是碎落的目光
什么时候一朵花深入内心
如经年失水的荆棘
什么时候那些皱纹散落成文字
写满窗台的凝思
在某个清晨你弯曲成通向的桥
任无数沉淀的脚印扩张
你只认识几张模糊的背影
就像随意堆积的秋天叶片
但具有诗意的死亡
走你的路　像一条孤独的蛇
你会渗透一切风景或忽略一切风景
这是另一个人看到的景场
你不会在乎　只记得一场雨的洗礼
一次风的袭击　一场干净的雪对你呈现的箴言
那么　你纯粹而直率
就像某些人眼中的窗玻璃
你贴在某个生活的角落　且行且远

Journey as We Continue

When did you forget that a road is no longer a road
Shattered by the shadowy gaze of eyes
When a flower walks into the mind
Like a dehydrated thorn
Wrinkles draw lines of words
Marking thoughts on the windowsill
One morning you bend into the shape of a bridge
Footsteps extending far and beyond
You only recognize a few blurry figures
A few random piles of fallen leaves
They may symbolize poetic death
The path you understand resembles a lone snake
You absorb the happenings, ignoring some
Such a scene is observed only by a third pair of eyes
You carry on, only to be reminded of the rain that baptized you
Or an attack by the wind
Or a snow that cleanses, all those metaphors
You hold onto this thing called integrity, like glass holding up a
    window
And you homestead right here, claiming your turf

第二辑　冬天的河流

PART 2 Rivers in the Winter

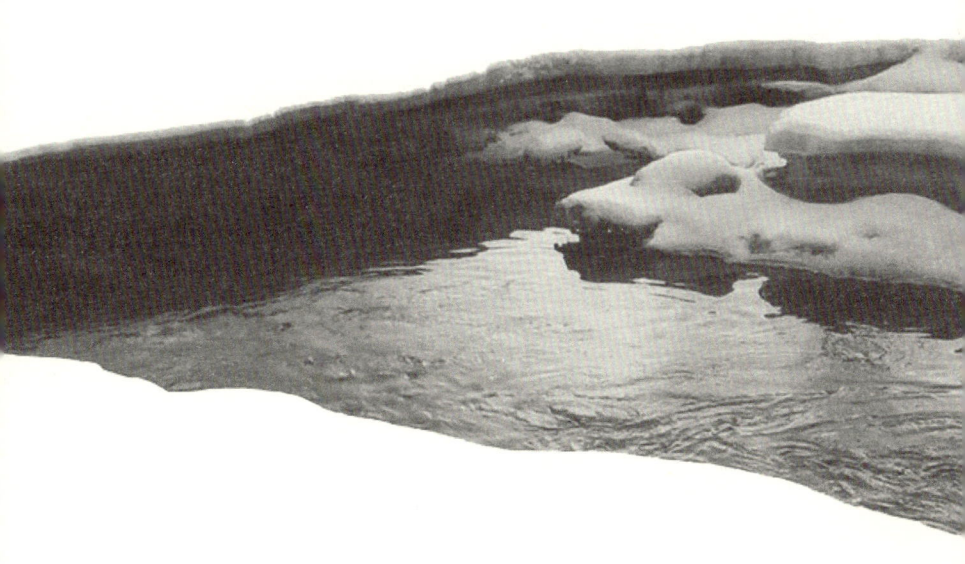

打开星星的光芒

河床

这曾经被水镌刻的底部
收藏沉思
你看见了它的皱纹
在老树根上缠绕
它的身体瘦成
坚持的石头和塞满水波的贝壳
现在　阳光翻晒一条船的骨架
天空暴露于干裂的缝隙
如果你还寻觅远去的流动
还在村庄寻找河流的故事
那么你必须敲打一首古老的民谣
古老的民谣在河床
多少年以前是风流的女子

Riverbed

This bed was carved by water
Sediments of thoughts
And the wrinkles you see, thin bodies
Wrapping around an old tree
Stubborn stones and sea shells filled with water
Now there is a skeleton of a boat, drying in the sun
The sky is exposed through cracks
If you are still looking for traces of departure
Or searching for river stories in the village
You should drill into an ancient folk song
Laying at the bottom of the river
Once upon a time, she was a lady of romance

打开星星的光芒

冰河

凝固的姿态　久远的记忆
你定格了某一瞬间厚度
白色火焰如原始的舞蹈
就像一群部落者的粗狂呐喊
在峡谷间突兀出永久的力度
我不确定你的未来
以此种形式的站立是旷古的
以此种形式的匍匐是对天空的对语
古老而单纯追求自身的怒放
释放自由天性的本质
任鹰撒播远方　任鹰解读生存
而这燃烧的河流
纯粹而坚毅
冰河　巨大的叶片
还是巨大水滴的延伸
或是一朵古老的神性花瓣
在你面前我失语
你似乎背负一个古老的使命
或呈现一种生命意义
我遇见你像一个小小的黑点
在你的纯色里感到卑微

Glacier

This solid state, memory from long ago
Resembles the thickness of one moment
White flames like the native's dance
A tribal man's chant
Between the valleys stands lasting strength
I am uncertain of your future
But such standing shall be timeless
Such crawling is a dialog with the sky
Ancient nobility in pursuit of self realization
Setting free truthfulness
Let this eagle travel far to spread a survivor's message
The river is on fire, with resolve and purity
Glacier, a gigantic leaf
A drop of water extending to infinity
A godly flower petal from ancient times
Before you I'm in awe and speechless
I see a continuing mission
And with regard to all life's significance
I am a speck under your eyes before your pure color
Deeply humbled

打开星星的光芒

暗流

你一生不曾看见
只有冷静中感觉
它在深远的地方　花朵也失落
歌声也会遥远
暗流　一切的阴暗的巢
孵化出一双手又一双手
隐秘的动作游移在手上　如隐蔽的刀子
不谋杀粮食和天空　这是它唯一的善良
它走在月亮的夜晚　风的夜晚
说出所有的枝柯都是预谋
它存在于平静的深夜　一朵花的内部
存在于一个春天或埋雷的季节
存在于一句话的背后
暗流　阴冷之姿
你一生都被牵扯或被猎杀

Unveiling the Star's Light

Undercurrent

You never saw it in your lifetime
Only sensing its clam formation
It's hidden in a deep place, where flowers are missing
Voices remote and faint
Undercurrent, nesting darkness
Incubating births by hands
Secret motion carried out by hand like a hidden knife
Kind enough not to lynch on sustenance and the sky
It walks in moonlit windy nights
Telling about sprigs' conspiracies
It breaths dark calm nights, inside a flower
It exists in spring or unsettling seasons
It hides behind words, cold and venomous
Involved with darkness, and chased after

打开星星的光芒

夜之风

夜行者掠走所有暴露的痕迹
也深入到你的体内
你在低处歌唱
你摸到它的力度
水在变形
暗夜之光正在变形
你感到正在变形的嘴巴
咬住白天的泡沫
它的牙齿深入
锋利的牙齿截获街灯的缝隙
这一切不为人所知
你只是感到远处也很近

Nightly Wind

A night stroller erases all traces
Enters your world unannounced
You are humming a tune, crouching low
You feel its power
Water is transformed
Light is transforming in the dark
And you feel your mouth undergoing transformation
Biting into the day's foam
With teeth clenching together
Sharp teeth clenching cracks in the street light
Oblivious to others
You feel close to the distant

打开星星的光芒

流凌

一首静默的歌词
多少年后依然让人无法张开嘴巴
无数影子在你尖顶破碎
而风携带着你的光芒
收藏天空
任黑夜与白天的堆积
你还是不动声色
你的内部有闪电和星光
是一首诗的进入
就像你的锋利牙齿咬住什么
山与更远的山在你背后
水与更远的水在你内心
这一切在你的深邃里
这一切在春天到来之前
我遇见了一次宏大的表演

Unveiling the Star's Light

Ice Run

Lines of lyrics in meditation
Unable to open their mouths after years of muteness
Many shadows fallen apart on your tip tops
Wind carries your color, collecting the sky
Dark nights piling on days
Superficial silence
Inside you is bountiful lightning and starlight
A poem is taking its place
As if sharp teeth bit into something
Mountains and farther mountains are behind you
Water and farther waters are inside you
In all your depths and widths, before the arrival of spring
There is an epic showcase

打开星星的光芒

黑夜正塌陷下来

云撕开了天空
巨大的裂缝在星星的悬崖上
谁砸疼了土地

此刻　土地是多么饥渴
在一块块石头上　承受
而星星的种子被大地聚融
那些隐藏的牙齿咬住根
咬住尘埃和一片片水域

此刻　我已是夜的碎片了
就在自己的影子里
听到了树木　花草的喊声

Unveiling the Star's Light

Dark Night Falling

Clouds tear open the sky
Cracking cliffs draped with stars
What falls on earth with painful injury?

Now the land is in tremendous thirst
Waiting on piles of stones
Seeds from the stars are fused with earth's soil
Invisible teeth hang onto the roots
And dust and water

Now I am a piece torn from the night
In my shadow
I hear cries of weeds and trees

打开星星的光芒

风不知道往哪边吹

山谷的风　田野的风　海上的风
还有一些无名的风和各种影子里的风
这些行走着的文字　捆起土地
奔向各自的方向

一浪高过一浪的喊声在空阔里
翻寻土地上的动静
而是什么突然地丢失
就像巨大的气流拥塞在出口
我听到了尖叫和碎裂声
而它们又像是一种道路　又被谁审视

Unveiling the Star's Light

Which Way the Wind Is Blowing

Valley wind, field wind, ocean wind
And unnamed, shadowy winds
Walking words
Picking up earth as they go

Cries echo, waves mount higher and higher
Digging up the soil, disturbing peace
Searching for the lost
An airy mass blocks all exits
I hear screaming and cracking
Or they are roads
Roads of another kind, never taken

而我，依然擎着一枚火把

什么文字能够撑起那种方向
我嫁接针芒上的光
在路上　卷起纯粹的月光
撩开遗失的梦　给浪尖上的风

我就坐在朽木上打开记忆
掰开泥水里的花语
带上鸽翅上的天空　夜晚和风暴
我就握紧黑色里的石头　做一次鉴别
那就先忘掉世上的颜色
在水凝注的神里　擎起火把
火把　照亮谁千年的骨头

Unveiling the Star's Light

Holding up a Torch

What words can shape a direction
I graft light from a needle's tip
On my way, I gather translucent moonlight
Breaking into lost dreams and sending them back to wind

Sitting on top of the putrefied wood
I dig up memories, decoding the stained flowers
Calling out to the sky where doves fly
And night and storm
A dark stone in my hand, I conduct a test
Letting go all worldly colors
And grabbing this torch, in the goddess of water
A torch, lighting up a road of thousand–year–old bones

打开星星的光芒

走吧——

山顿悟了万年　水漂流了万年
风也撞出了夕阳的血
还有翘首的黑夜　把自己装载在星星上
大地在光里燃烧出花朵的思绪

走吧——
不要说荒芜的家园还在翅膀上盘旋
不要说路上还有无形的墙
不要说路上的荆棘刺痛了天空
我们就踏着叶子上的沉思
走吧　在夜色飘落之时刚好上路

Let's Go

For ten thousand years
The mountains sat and waters flowed
Wind crashing into the sun, bleeding
Yearnings of dark nights, fantasies for the stars
Earth engulfed in the flames of an old sage's wreath

Let the journey begin
Don't say that the deserted homeland still circles in the air
Don't say there are invisible walls along the way
And thorns piercing the sky
We shall step over the fallen leaves
Let's go
As time is perfect
When the night is falling

打开星星的光芒

冰的行走方式

冰在零度时醒了
它走在星星的注目里
风使它站立得更高
它的行走在你触及它时就感到了
它盘爬在你的体内
有一种刺痛让你颤动
让你感到一种沉静下的力量
很多时候你都会被它击败
你都不会忘记一块冰的行走方式
沉默得尖锐

How Ice Walks

Ice awakes above zero
It walks under the stars' gaze
Wind pushes it to stand taller
You feel its motion with a simple touch
It is crawling inside you
A sharp pain jolts you awake
And you maintain your composure
Many times you feel defeated
Yet never forget how an ice walks
Silent, yet with resolve

打开星星的光芒

河流的目光

我或许会替代河流,保持着一种弯度
我的弯度是谁在最初拉起弓一样的力度
山在我的注视里,家园在我的注视里
河流,是谁古老的放置,像一个人的目光
它的穿过也背负天空的光芒,土地捆绑的深夜
它的穿过使历史凸起,纷纷落定的文字,像一具瓷器
它的穿过有竹简上的影子,是夏天叶子翻卷出沉淀的闪电
而此种目光还要接近什么?一粒沙子也持久于岸上

不息的河流,可触摸的目光
这是谁走进土地时把内心给了世界
我感到月光的漂泊,在你目力中映出的又一种梦境
是否是你,给我一次远行的验证
还有鸟群衔来的早晨、黄昏,那么质感地驻留在你背上
一次次让我反复唱颂身边的村庄、城市
是否是你的初愿
我身埋在一种精神的高度
在一个个冷静的午夜,想象成一块小小石子敲打你

Unveiling the Star's Light

现在,我感到了你目光的迫近
几乎倾斜着身子与自己对语
几乎怀疑起你存留的目的,就是让我重新认识什么
现在,我感到你深处的弯弯曲曲,像一根透亮的绳子
你要捆绑起什么?你的鱼群古往今来地穿梭
你的鱼群喋喋不休地说出什么
你转过多少弯才能得到证明
而你这不败落的目光,别人感觉不到的目光
把树木的身子染起颜色,把我居住的家园染起颜色
把一切让你关注的染起颜色,而你要点燃什么
亿万年的等待,你替代谁的出现
或许某一天,我会是你身边的一枚聆听的贝壳
也会被你看到,与你一起汇合的日子

打开星星的光芒

Gaze of a River

Perhaps I will become a sinuous river
As tight as a bow being pulled
Mountains in my view, and land of my home
River, placed here in ancient times, gazing through a peculiar eye
You carry the glory of the sky, and the dark night swaddled by earth
Running through time, with twists and turns
Scattering words, like shattered porcelain
Image of old bamboo books, summer thunder bolts
River's gaze. A sand grain taking a permanent place on the shore

River's unstoppable flow, where eyes meet
Someone walking into the land with a heart for the world
I feel moonlight drifting, reflecting a dream scene in your eyes
Is it you, testifying to me before a long journey
Dawn and dusk on the beaks of birds, landing solidly on my back
With resounding odes to the villages and towns
Could that be what you wished for from the beginning
I become invisible with soaring spirit
Such a calm night, an imaginary stone is knocking on you

Unveiling the Star's Light

Now I feel your eyes on me, leaning your body for a dialogue
Why do you stay, and what do you want me to learn again?
Now I see deep in you all the twists and bends, like a translucent rope
What are you tying with it? Schools of fish swim
Chatter incessantly about how many turns to make to be approved
And your undefeated look, undetectable by others
Is dyeing the trees their colors, dyeing your home to meet a code
Dyeing all you care into their true colors
Who are you trying to enlighten
Billions of years have passed by and who are you representing
Perhaps someday I will become a sea shell leaning on your side
 listening
Perhaps you will notice me, and our lives will merge

打开星星的光芒

没有冻伤的鸟鸣

事物的行走都慢下来
事物像一棵树木抱紧了自己
在空阔中　石头都像凸显的伤口
而没有冻伤的是一个早晨的鸟鸣
鸟鸣鲜亮得像隐藏的花瓣　开在窗外
我不知道她象征了什么
只是在冬天的寒气中唱着
我虽没有走进透亮的音节
可我在她叫声里获得一种生命
在沉寂的时候　谁还在洗着我的眼睛

Unveiling the Star's Light

Bird's Chirping Unharmed

All movements slow down
Everything holds tight like a tree trunk
From space, stones resemble protruding wounds
Bird's morning chirping unharmed by frost
Bright sound sharp like invisible flower petals
Blooming outside the windows
I don't know what the song symbolizes
Breaking free the freezing winter
Unable to see through those bright notes
But I reclaim my life hearing the songs
In my solitude, someone does cleansing for my eyes

打开星星的光芒

开在寒风中的花

我始终叫不出她的名字
我始终在她姿态中走不出来
她占据了我整个冬天
她是谁　小小的灯盏照亮了这个世界
小小的灯盏在一步之遥生动
也许她不为谁而来
只想让寒风再雕琢些什么
这是我感到的　并带上她内心的颜色

Flowers Blooming in Chilly Wind

I can never remember her name
She is captured in her state of mind, unable to escape
She takes part my entire winter
Who is she, a small lamp lighting up the whole world
Bright light within reach
Perhaps she is here without a purpose
She only beckons the cold wind
To keep on coming, along with her colored flames

打开星星的光芒

一汪静水

它一直在我的左边
不住地增长
一些新的元素每天都漫过我的眼前
止于一种沉静
它是劳累的,有深夜里的思绪,黎明的思考
它是孤独的,有我岁月的碎片
也是永远的,就像另一只眼,看着我的额际一年年扩展
它的中央沉淀着许多只手,道路和一些高高低低
它神情淡然,水波不兴
它的深邃里储存着许多翅膀和一些声音
我每次走进时都会看到那种亲切,比血还浓
我每次都会抚摸它的深度,甚至高过我的年轮
不知它是否抽离了我身体的一部分
那种坦然比天空还淡定
只有此时,我才会低吟起一首古老的歌
如同把自己放进去,与水亲和

它是我放心不下的

每天夜晚我都走去放置体内的荒芜
我都会静静地坐下，收藏起一些什么
我就坐在那里，让自己成为水
手臂成为一棵树木，心的鸟飞过，不留下远方
它就安静在左边，像我生命的营寨
有时候就安扎在一朵云上，看着沸腾着的土地

打开星星的光芒

A Pond of Still Water

It has stayed on my left side
Unceasingly rising
New elements float to my eyes each day
And then stay still in silence
It is hardworking, packing thoughts to the night and dawn
It is lonely, like a piece broken off from life
It is eternal, another eye witnessing my forehead
Broadening year after year
And there are many hands in the water, and bumpy roads
Calm with tiny ripples
And it holds folded wings and voices
Whenever I approach it I sense affectionate warmth
Blood thicker than water
My hand senses its depth, more aged than my rings
And I wonder if it would consider me a part of its own
With its detached and relaxed appearance, like a sky
I know when I am inside it I will recall an old song
Submerging myself entirely and bonding with liquid

Unveiling the Star's Light

There is a concern for it growing in me, that I must
Put myself inside its body to relieve the worries
I would sit quietly, gathering what comes to me
I would sit there till I liquefy into puddles
My arms become a tree, birds flying over and departing

It would always be on my left side, like a home base
And sometimes it floats above a cloud
Watching over a turbulent landscape

独坐江岸

我比黄昏还安静,像一块石头
云翻卷出内心的文字
我似乎是辽远的一部分或者一次等待
在天空的缝隙里,读星星下的背影
我似乎寻找一次涨潮的约定
在隐约的声音里要辨别灯塔照亮的内涵
而黑夜埋不住渔火和唱晚的歌
此时,我像黑色之花开放在浪尖
在一次次进入岸堤时,那种撞击力消逝在高大的楼顶
有一种可能的破碎,像收敛的余辉
这个时候,谁模糊了我,一只鸟啁啾而过

一只鸟啁啾而过
我的独坐也模糊了体内的象征
在风吹过衣角时折起了谁的皱纹
并被宽大的江面扩张
一直被那只不眠的行船带走
此时,我的安静不被自己了解了

Unveiling the Star's Light

　　我看着远处的灯火，依靠背后的城市
　　目光一滴滴掉落，垒筑的江岸越来越高
　　越来越高的是我说不出的，风拂过心间的沙粒

打开星星的光芒

Loner by the River Bank

Quieter than twilight, like a stone
Cloud rolling out its voice
I am in a faraway land, waiting
Between the cracks of the sky, I read behind the stars
Searching high tides
Distant voice, telling the story of a light house
Darkness doesn't hide the fisherman's fire and night songs
Now, I bloom like a dark flower on tips of waves
Time and time again crashing against the river bank
Smashing sound vanishing through tall ceilings
Like sunlight scattering into infinite pieces
Now this softens me like a chirping sound from distance

A bird flies over chirping
A lone sitter softens his symbols inside the body
Wind blows over, flapping corners of my clothes
Wrinkles, who do they belong to
Rippling across the face of the river

Unveiling the Star's Light

And collected by the sleepless boat
Why do I sit here all alone?
Watching the lights far away, leaning on a city behind me
I drop my gaze as the river bank rises
Higher and higher beyond my words
And I wait for the wind to put a new layer
Over the sand dunes

打开星星的光芒

我的沉思被一块石头占有

是的 我每天都掀开一张文字
我必须驻足在某些必然的事件上
自然的　人为的　似乎都陷入一面镜子里
连同我也被照出细节
而每一个文字都是一把钥匙　能打开多少隐藏的门

我的沉思被一块石头占有
我感到那种沉默就是一种语言
它在忽略里　在看见时就搬不开了
而石头却时刻拯救着我的思路

现在我必须通过一场雨验证它
那些凝固了的雨点还闪烁着光芒
比星星神秘　比我早年丢掉的眼泪更值得抚摸
我接近它时　感到天空的空寂
石头是否在某个时间也种植了一种道路
现在我敲打着寻找　在它缄默里把一生的话语拿走
把唯一能接触到内层的思想点燃

而这是一颗什么样的种子
让大地凸起　似乎掩藏了喑哑
我必须在风吹起大片颜色时得到启示
抵达你沉实的思想　融合到我内心
或许是一片荒芜中被野兽叼走的真实
或许是它在一个深夜获取生命的原始
而这是怎样的石化的种子
我的抚摸冰凉　我的抚摸有历史的厚度
其实我一直在学着石头　让水冲刷　让阳光照耀

今天　我必须得到验证
我必须抵达它忘却的文字
把它移植到能生长出想象的地方
它曾经的想象是否延续到我梦中的河流
而这是什么样的种子　它是否还在潜行
它的声音在哪里　它替代了谁的身份
当我在一幅幅画中看到它　在路上遇见它
当我看见那些天上的星星时　已经若有所得

打开星星的光芒

Thoughts Seized by a Stone

Each day I turn a page for new words
And pause to ponder those inevitable events
Naturally those incidents fall inside a mirror
Reflecting details concerning me
Every word becomes a key to a hidden door

My thoughts are taken over by a stone
Silence is its language
In neglect, it loses its mobility
Yet you are my constant rescuer when I am lost in thinking

Now I must prove this through rain
Solidified rain drops still gleam
More mysterious than stars
Worthier of my touch than the tears I shed
Close up I feel the emptiness of the sky
Stone becomes a road in due time
Now I knock on its silence to relieve my own words

Unveiling the Star's Light

To ignite the thoughts deep inside

This must be a seed, but of what kind
Nubs of the earth, shields to mute voice
I must read its sign when the wind blows
Patches of colors flying in the wind
Arriving with a state of mind, befitting the heart
It must be the truth taken by beasts in the wilderness
It must be the reason to render new lives in dark nights
Majestic petrified seeds
I feel the coolness, touching the depth of time
And I shall follow you to give myself to the rain
And let the sun shine all over me

Today I must acquire a testimony
I must reach its forgotten words
And transplant them into earth where imagination grows
Like grafting an old vision to a new dream
What a seed, still in camouflage
What does its voice embody?
When I see it in paintings, or run into it on the road
And when I see stars covering the nightly sky
I shall have the answers

第三辑_雪落有声

PART 3 Sound of Snow Falling

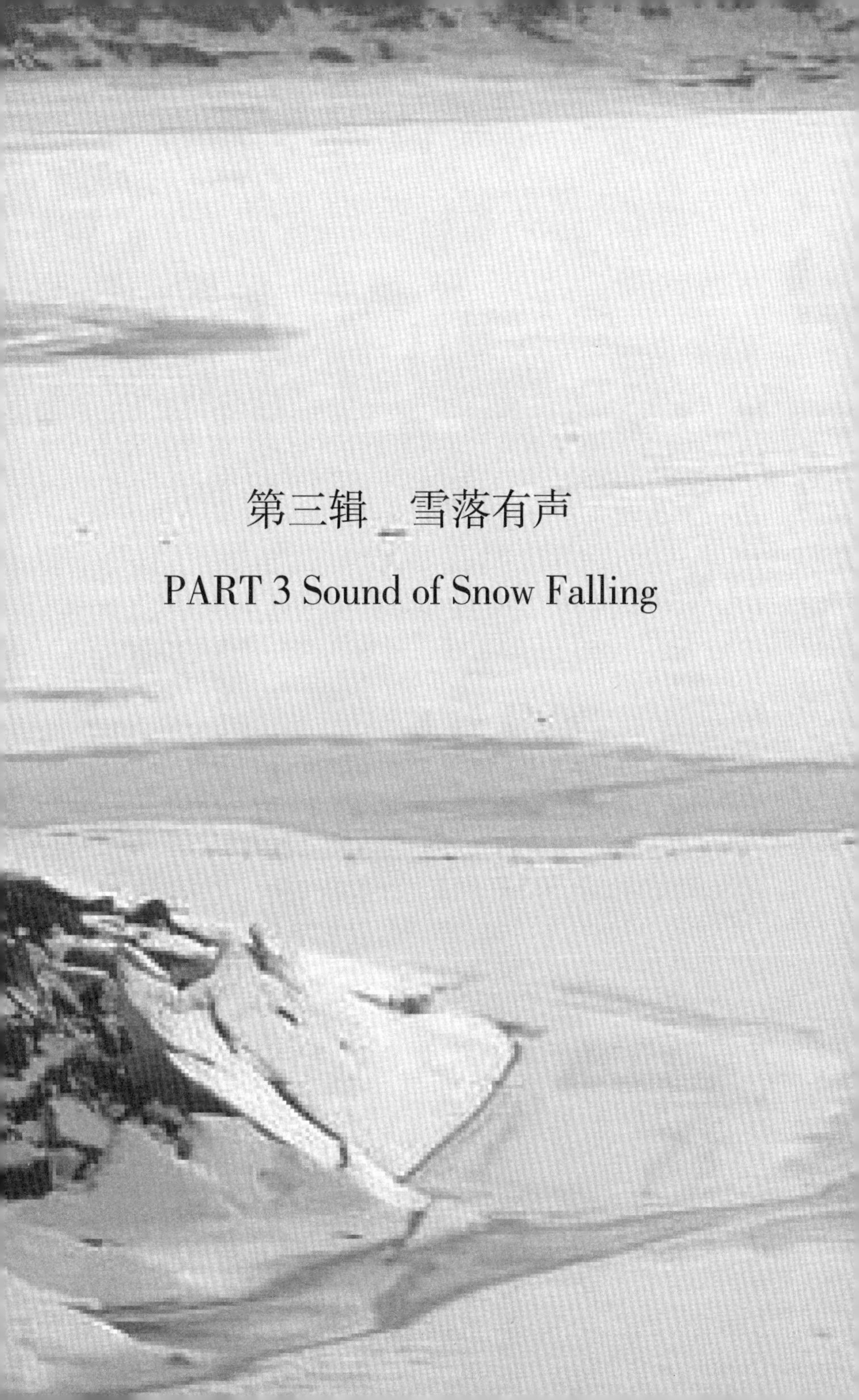

打开星星的光芒

一盏太阳的橘灯

雾埋住了江水的声音
江水在雾里是一条蛇的皮
我感到了一种暗藏的挣扎
这时候　我看见了一盏橘灯
橘灯　橘灯　在雾间穿行
就像谁在提着一团黄色的火焰
这么好看的火焰散在雾气里
一瓣一瓣　落在一座城市的楼角
还有许多窗儿　正被点燃

The Orange Light of the Sun

Fog silences river's voice
River runs like a floating snake skin
Hiding its struggle
Now there is an orange light, permeating the fog
A yellow fire, glowing through the air
Petals, one after another, fall throughout the city
Lighting up the windows

打开星星的光芒

打开冬天的记忆

像一瓣雪掠过窗户
也是我的失眠
在小小的北风里变换托腮的姿势
而我的想终不能打败一个冬天
就在台灯下沉静成一枚冰凌
暂时把他的名字收藏
不知从什么时候起　我面朝北方
描摹一座半岛的模样
不知从什么时候起　我开始走失
就像冬夜的草睡在星星里
就在今夜吧　把思念拉到文字里
铺成弯弯的小路　这样就不怕冻伤

Awaken Winter's Memories

A snowflake skips outside the window
And so does my insomnia
Tossing and turning
The north wind switching hands to prop up my chin
Meditation can't beat the season
But it can help an icicle hung on the edge of a lamp
Let it have no name for the time being
Then I find myself facing the north
With a clear vision of a peninsula
I am lost but not unconscious
Like winter grass napping in the stars
Tonight, I turn yearning into words
Lay them on a curvy path
And there would be no frostbites

打开星星的光芒

雪落有声

那纯粹的质地是凝聚的一个个呐喊
当你陷入静谧中的洪大
那些从隐秘的远方传来的声音
打开另一层空间
这是你无法遇见的事情
雪朵瞬间开败，它的声音进入不防之地
让你在恍惚中失去眼前的事物
如同这个现有的世界
一半在雪之上，一半被雪声掩埋
你发现沉埋你年轮的雪线渐渐变黑
那些经年的声响遁迹
而你无法掌握雪朵之重
在它翻动天空的时候，还有许多美丽的压迫

Sound of Snow Falling

Your substance is solidified with cries
When you fall into this soundless space
The voices arrive from hidden places far away
Entering into a new space
Such encounter you may never have
Snow buds blossom and wither in an instant
Sound falling in the unexpected ears
Making you lose yourself in confusion
Just like the world in front of you
Half above snow, half buried
You realize that the growth rings turn dark in the snow
The sound of the past fades away
Unable to gauge the weight of the snow blossoms
When they stir up the sky
So much oppressed beauty

打开星星的光芒

雪的重量

你会看见雪不仅压弯目光
也会压弯一条河，压弯一群人的声音
那些白色火苗之上的力量
正一点点滴下来，不经意间砸疼你的手指
雪的重量就在你眉宇间伺机
而你无法收集起雪落之声
就像你无法阻止那些旺盛的白色火苗
进入事物的内部
就在这一瞬间，你不知道发生了什么
你看见的只是那些张开的嘴巴
那些嘴巴说不出雪的背后

Unveiling the Star's Light

Weight of the Snow

The snow bends the onlookers
It bends the river, deforming voices
Magic rising from the while flames
Falling onto my fingers, pain felt
Snow amasses between my brows
But I cannot make it stay, the sound of the snow falling
Just as you are unable to stop those vigorous flames from
Entering the inner part of things
In an uncounted instant
Mouths become wide open, flabbergasted
Unable to say what it is behind such harsh falling

打开星星的光芒

雪域

雪域比纸更超然
它上面很多圈圈点点
你不会明白圈点的是土地还是海水
你只知道雪线很远,远得天空是一只翅膀
这时,你就像在城堡中,你不是童话故事的主人公
你只是在清晰地看自己的倒影
是有许多城墙堆垒的
这些暗藏的城墙就在被雪线圈点的地方
那些纯粹的雪线,比阴影更可怕
它让你看见阳光中密密麻麻的词语
飘过雪顶,然后戳疼你黑色的瞳孔
这是你真实的体验,你独立其间,世间茫茫

Unveiling the Star's Light

Snow Field

This snow field is more detached than paper
With many circles and dots
You won't know whether these are fields or oceans
You only know the snow lines reach far, like a wing in the sky
Now you are in a fortress, not a legendary princess
Except you see clearly your own shadow inside the walls
Walls of the snow lines' hidden borders
More terrifying than shadows are those pure snow lines
You see packed words in sunlight
Flying over the snow, dashing with pain into your eyes
This is a true experience, as you stay in solitude
In a vast field of snow

打开星星的光芒

雪的背后是湿地

湿地从雪内心显现出来
更像真实的云影
当你小心走过
像走过一段人生的过程
其实这块湿地很干燥
就像火燃烧过的痕迹
但你看不见灰迹
你看见的是一片一片有声有色的记忆
记忆无论给谁,谁都会纪念
就像你无意中得到什么
你会记住小小的湿地,小小美好的阴影
假设你的生活是一堆雪
那化解的是你自己身体某一部位
你或许这个时候会惊醒
或者在你生活的布影上裁剪什么,其实都是流逝
这个时候你还会想到很多
比如,一栋房子被无情化解,一座村庄被化解
一块争抢的土地被化解
其实始终有一座雪山,虽然你感慨得很轻很轻
但它的领地无限扩张,你与你们都会被围剿
这些雪后边的湿地,正隐隐涨大的潮水
始终高过你的视线

Unveiling the Star's Light

Wetland Behind the Snow

Wetness pierces through the snow
Truthful like clouds
As if it was walking through a journey of life
But this wetland lacks water, parched with burns
Though you don't see the ashes
You see patches of vivid memories
Memorial for any and all that went through here
You happen to remember this tiny wetland
A small piece of shadowy beauty
Imagine your life as a pile of snow
And your body melting away
You may be jolted awake right now
Or perhaps you are busy tending the backdrop
Watching time unfolding
You envision a house that's melting away
A village vanishing
Sought-after land disappearing, far and near
But there will always be snow mountains, as light as you feel them
Expanding, surrounding you and all of you
The wetland behind the snow, silently expanding to form a high tide
Higher than your eyes can reach

雪花　一瓣瓣月光

飘舞着　莅临与我有关的冬天
纷飞着　触摸与我有关的天空
宁静的白　填充树木和一片空阔的愿望
这些生动的说不出来的心灵呓语
在一夜之间鲜活成一瓣瓣月光
遇见了这个深夜和我

雪花　我还是踩碎了你拢起的心镜
在你照进一段路途和一座城市之时
我无法看清那些事物的表情
只是在你的身后感觉一些变化
我只是在雪花微弱的光里验证自己
而你不知要停留在什么地方或谁的内心

Unveiling the Star's Light

Snowflakes, Petals of the Moon

Dancing, here you come cheering me and this winter
Flying, touching the sky and me
Quietly, such paleness, between woods and sky
Fulfilling wishes
Such liveliness, sweet voice of the soul
Petals of the moonlight, babies born at night
Arriving to meet me and darkness

Snowflakes, I step on you and break you
Leading you to a path towards the city
I can't tell the things we encounter and their expressions
Only perpetual changes as I follow
And test myself as I'm lit and led by your light
Will you settle somewhere and whose heart will you melt?

打开星星的光芒

树上盛开着雪意

这是哪些鸟在奔飞时依存的羽毛
早晨也思考在树上
有一些落下来　有一些还保持欲飞姿势
有一些飘进风里　有一些被阳光燃烧

我与树之间有一尺之遥
于雪意烘托的地方
有许多小小的影子与我紧紧挨着
我感到了又一种飞
感到树与我一样的心境走过早晨

Unveiling the Star's Light

Snow Perching on the Tree

What kind of bird are you with feathers like this
Like morning thoughts landing on sprigs
Some falling and some flying
Some blown in the wind
Yet others catching fire in the sun

I am an arm away from the tree
Such a place of snow sighting
Tiny shadows lean close towards me
I sense another kind of flying
This tree and I share a journey
Through this snowy morning

打开星星的光芒

一处草地被一场雪释解

一处草地走到这里就沉静了
现在　雪下的草地是它自己的
它在想着自己的草　没去想一座城市的样子
它正看见自己的脚印在一场雪里

这是白天　草地正怀揣自己的天空
它在雪的下面放开自己
而谁也没有关注它是多么的真实
它正在忘记夏天的闪电　一片云语
它正在一枚种子的内心　放牧思绪

A Lawn Interpreted by Snow

A lawn turns quiet when it gets here
It returns to itself when covered in snow
Being nothing but grass, no part of the city
Simply watching the snow leaving footprints

In the daylight the lawn has the sky in its lap
Blooming under the snow cover
This truth goes unnoticed
Summer thunder and lightning are being forgotten
And so are the wordy clouds
The lawn is focusing life inside a grass seed
A seed sprouting into a prairie

打开星星的光芒

雪影

是谁的身子闪过窗户
是谁没留下目光就走远
是谁让我坐定一个下午也打不开
小小的雪影与世界擦肩而过

我多么想看到更多的雪影留驻人间
多么想挽留此种飘逸
它带着天空的颜色
天空的颜色纯净到我的眸子　我会多么生动

Unveiling the Star's Light

Shadow of the Snow

A figure flashing by me
Without a pause or even concerned look
Who anchored me to this chair in the afternoon
Shadows of the snow and the world missed each other as they went by

How I wish to see a marking left by the shadows
And to savor this wild drift
Hold colors of the sky in my palm
Such pure colors, shone from the eyes
And everything becomes so alive

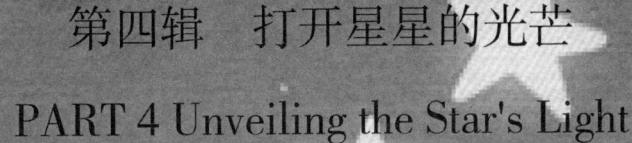

第四辑 打开星星的光芒

PART 4 Unveiling the Star's Light

打开星星的光芒

那片海

那片海蓝得群鸟乱了天空
那片海一直于我指尖荡开
很多时候　我把海塞进沉默里
有时候也把海反过来　看看鸟隐藏起的饥饿

这是迷人的海
它蓝得深沉　蓝成一个巨大的花朵
在它翻卷的花瓣上　有夜晚的香　白天的香
这么一片海闪现在我指尖
对谁开放

Unveiling the Star's Light

This Ocean

The ocean's blue rivals the sky
Confused birds, in all directions, fly
It spreads out between my fingers
I find it in a place of silence, many times
And sometimes I turn it upside down
Watching the birds hiding underneath in hunger

This majestic ocean, charming
A giant indigo flower
Deep petals thrashing fragrant scent of the night
Aroma in the sun
Gleaming on my fingertips
But for whom does the blossom yearn?

象征

如果我能找到它
就先背负一个存在的意义
就像无语的大海
如果我能看见它
必须燃烧一生的沉静
如同一朵旷野上的菊

或许它陈旧如石　新鲜如日
或许我一生都走不进去
而它的光环足让黑夜沉到大地的梦中

Symbols

I allow its preemptive existence
Before I find it
Like a mute ocean, to see it I must
Burn out the silence of its life
Like a lone chrysanthemum a wild field

Aged as a stone, or fresh like the moon
Perhaps I will never be immersed in
Yet his rings so bright, sinking the night sky
Into dreams of the earth

打开星星的光芒

走进一滴雨

我看见它时　听见声音的膨胀
许多挣扎的影子碎了
而一滴雨还沿自己的轨迹行走
忽略尘埃的叫嚣　越来越透明
我就在此种光亮里　撞见天空的姿势
在措手不及之时　感到了疼痛

Walking into a Drop of Rain

When I see it, I hear sound expanding
Broken shadows struggling
One drop dragging alongside its path
Ignoring cries of the dust, increasingly transparent
In such brightness, accidental encounter with the sky
Unprepared, I feel the pain

打开星星的光芒

水边的舞蹈

浪尖上的鱼鹰在舞蹈
啄破黄昏的鱼鹰在舞蹈
低低的像灰色的云片
我似乎看见它体内的雨
它携带着箭入水中
体内的雨谁去触摸

这是水边的舞蹈
胜过风中奔走的花朵
胜过夕阳燃烧的那块铁
火光中溅出的灰色小小火星
有一种力量穿透河流
它的翅膀在收割水上沉淀下来的灿烂
它在收割水上一座城市撕掉的碎片

鱼鹰,又是谁的碎片
它在追随波涛
波涛之上的小小足尖蘸满江河的语言

它在追随最后的余晖,水边的余晖
能给它多少捕捉
我感到它凝重中持有的词语
似乎要在落日最后的回望中获得什么

鱼鹰起伏于远远近近
似乎要啄破我眸子里的光
要独占我与整个的旷野
翅膀拍打着越来越深的暮色
它在暮色里沉潜
就像在另一种水中要抓取什么

鱼鹰掠过沙子上的光
掠过一座旷野上的光
它在第一颗星子出现的地方舞蹈
它在掉进水里的城市上空舞蹈

这融合了黑夜的碎片
让我看不见被翅膀穿行的空间
突然沉静得不知所措
这些都在鱼鹰的脊背上
这些都被鱼鹰一个个塞进水里
此时,我感到这种方式替代了我手上的沉重
它要携带我在走远的浪尖上放牧

打开星星的光芒

A Dance by the Water

Cormorants dancing on the tips of waves
Beaks pecking at dusk, dancing cormorants
Grey clouds hovering low
Streaks of rain inside their body
Like arrows shot into water
Who is there to feel the rain

This dance, stronger than flowers in the wind
Hotter than iron heated at sunset
Grey sparkles flying off the fire
Forces strung along the river
Wings harvest sediments of light at the river bottom
And gather torn pieces of the city

Cormorants, broken pieces flying
Chasing the waves
Webbed feet dabbed with river words
Chasing sunset by the water

Unveiling the Star's Light

Scraping up last reflections
I sense the weight of those words hung on their feet
As you turn around gazing, such thoughtfulness at sunset

Cormorants far and near, gliding
As if to peck into the light in my eyes
As if to investigate my world and this wilderness
Wings flapping in the evening as it gets darker
Immersing in the colors of dusk
Another water world, you keep on catching

Cormorants stirring radiance in sand
Gathering light over the fields
Dancing where the first star shines
Above the sunken city in the water

You merge broken pieces with the dark night
Leaving invisible space between the wings
Now silence descends with uneasiness
Riding on the spines of the birds, diving back to the water
And this motion erases weight on my fingertips
Taking me to the tip of the waves to be a herdsman

打开星星的光芒

独占的旷野

我要摘下果实里的秘密
收下草地里的秘密
我要打开野花盛开的秘密
一个大旷野在鹰翅上的苍茫
一个旷野走进树木里的深度
我要翻耕泥土里古老的声音
翻耕高高的天空
我要所有进入草尖上的风都敞开胸襟
要所有的颜色来涂抹我内心的诗

我安静地看着远与自己
看着群鸟奔飞在目光里的姿势
看着那些沉思默语的石头呈现什么状态
那些被风磨砺过的皱纹
那些被云丝淋漓写意的皱纹
那些被旷野卷帘过风暴的皱纹
在什么时间凸现一幅油画
让我走进去轻轻放置思考

Unveiling the Star's Light

　　轻轻把一个涨满风与光的土地举得高高

　　此时，我是风中的蝴蝶了
　　我翩然走过高高低低
　　我埋藏干净的文字于花蕊
　　埋藏起语言的意义于潮湿
　　我翩然如蝴蝶，在闪电解读过的高地
　　在雨水冲刷过的沟壑
　　在城市还没涉足的地方
　　我轻轻盛开内心，像蓝色花朵，朝向海的背负

　　我站立在旷野，独立的影子，风吹不动
　　我占有的旷野都拥进旷古的沧桑
　　我站着，替代另一个我
　　交出黑暗，交出被城市泡制的岁月
　　交出一首未完成的诗

打开星星的光芒

Wilderness Field

I carve out the secrets in the fruits
Harvesting them in haystacks
Unveiling those enclosed in the blossoms
Empty fields on the wings of eagles
Wilderness spreading in the deep forest
I dig up old sounds in the soil
Tilling the sky high above
I beckon wind to spread grass tips
I invite color to smear on my poems

I watch soundless faraway land and absorb
How birds run in the eyes of an observer
Silent stone beholds its state of mind
Wrinkles sharpened by wind
And wrinkles worn by shreds of clouds
And those surviving rolling storms in the wild
An oil painting appearing in time
And now I walk inside, pondering in silence

Unveiling the Star's Light

As I raise the land with my eyes
So full with wind and light, higher and higher

A butterfly I shall become in the wind
Sailing through wuthering heights
Hiding innocent words inside flowers
Messaging the lines into a blur
Fluttering butterfly over heights stroked by lightning
Gulches carved by rains
Virgin island unseen by the city
I open, ever so softly, an indigo orchid facing the back of the sea

As I stand here with my shadow in solitude, stand still in the wind
This wilderness beholds a long past
As I am here standing in place of another selfness
I turn over the darkness, the manufactured city life
And surrendering this poem, unfinished

打开星星的光芒

与诗有关

1. 春

如果你相信眼睛
有一种睡眠也会开放
雨中的花朵　大海
你只会偶然发现那种生存的意义
待你去寻觅不动声色的阴影
阴影会比山与水爬得高
比风还要突然
你在一处待久了会体味到隐秘的春天
搅乱了泥土以及望远
其实这些都与诗有关
诗在春天可以生发任何事物
也可以让你坐在边缘地带像一株树
你要准备伸出很多的手——

Concerning Poetry

Spring

If you believe in your eyes
Sleepiness will blossom
Flowers in the rain, the sea
How significant that type of living
Waiting for you to notice wordless shadows
Shadows growing higher than rivers and mountains
And sharper than wind
You will encounter a hidden spring after some living
Disturbing land and its future
All these have to do with poetry
Poetry grows unexpected freshness in spring
And you can sit on the edge like a tree, ready at anytime
Reaching out your multiple hands

2. 夏

最好你先要接受一次洗礼
那不是这个季节普通的雨场
你必须经过一次雷声　不是一般的雷
还必须体验一种风沙的袭击
当然不是你看到的姿势
这些现场都是你生命的必经之路
夏天　使你无处躲藏
很多草都会抽出你身体的某一部位
使你无法选择地暴露在欲望或沉思之中
但是　只要小心
你不会转到一朵花或河流的背面
你只要细心就会发现许多微妙的空间正在缩小
正在挤你的身体
使你有一种痛感　像拔节的笋　无法预想
还有更多的现象　比如一群麻雀　几只穷飞的鸟
都会全心地接近夏之腹地
它们需要的是摆脱饥饿
它们很单纯　不像你
你只需要对方　不管对方是不是一个夏天灌满的水
你始终要打捞些什么

Summer

You must undergo a baptism
Not just any rain of the season
You must undergo thunder in flames
Against attack by sand storms
Of unpredictable patterns and forms
Truthful encounters as in life
Inevitable, no where to hide
Grass extracts part of your body
Exposing your desire as you become bare
Yet with care you will not turn to the dark side
The back side of a flower, or a river going upstream
The tiny space is shrinking on you
Pushing your body to feel the pain like bamboo going through
Unexpected growth spurts
Phenomenon like a flock of sparrows flying over endless skies
All approaching the bottom of the season
Just to escape hunger – such an innocent purpose
Unlike you, oblivious of the water level
Still try to catch what it may hold

打开星星的光芒

3. 秋

只需要一种果实就代表你已接受了秋天
秋天装在自己的口袋
或眸子间或蛙鸣的声震里
你只要多走一步就会感到老辣的荆棘正与你对峙
还有更多的草　它们的背正在弯曲
它们正要通过你说出海阔天空
这时　你不需要多想
只要一个眼神便不会忘记那些土地上的负重
被一枚苹果　橘子或者向日葵摘走象征
留下的只有暗喻　这个时候你只需要暗喻
你只缄默地携带这些与生俱来的东西
走进一片野地或野地经久的一处黑夜
你会感到有一种别样的海　很壮阔
只是你永远不了解那处海洋会慢慢走远
只会携带你的十指交到别处验证

Autumn

You need one fruit to know you have harvested
Autumn in your pockets
In your eyes, or by the sound of loud frogs
Up close you feel the thorns pointing at you
And grass bent over backwards
They are telling you about the vast sky
You need only one glance to know
The weight carried by the land
The symbol of an apple, of an orange, or sunflowers
Only allusion, and that is the only thing you need now
To carry with your such silent gifts bestowed at birth
Walking into wilderness
A corner echoing darkness in the field
You will see a different ocean of magnificence
Only you don't realize that this sea will drift away
Taking all your fingers and toes

4. 冬

你看见雪花时就像捕捉到了纯粹的影子
这些东西慢慢铺盖赤裸的大地
大地上就像一团冻结的太阳光芒
唯独你还站在雪地寻找什么
就像一块掩埋半截身子的石头
只暴露出一段黑影
它的冷就像你的手指
世界需要这样　需要半截石头的暴露
或手指
这些都被一个很冷的夜晚发现
冰凌上挂着谁穿过的鞋子
这个时候　季节不生长
只有标记或者你纸上的文字不小心走下来
丢下一串脚印与天空对语

Winter

The snowflakes you see are shadows you catch
Slowly blanketing the bare ground
The ground is frozen, and so are the sunbeams
As you search in the snow
Like a stone half buried, exposing half a dark figure
Freezing like your finger tips
This world needs half exposed stones or fingers
That pay attention to chilling nights
Worn shoes hung on icicles
A season when nothing grows
Only signs, or the words on paper fall off occasionally
Leaving a string of footprints
In dialogue with the grey sky

5. 天

它很大
你无法抓到它的一角
你只好待在一处　像一棵试图突围冬天的草
你只看见那些云片　像你身上的衣服
穿一件换一件
样式不一　只装饰
你的装饰是一种可能
天空无法装饰
只能靠想象　云片不过是脚印
不知道是谁的徘徊
或许是文字背后的意义
这种形象的东西只让你再次猜测
就像你猜测天空是什么一样
你一辈子都猜不透
它只给你一面　就像镜子
你永远站不到它的背后
你只是扮演了一棵试图突围冬天的草
看着那阔远的蓝或者灰　而你会被理解

Sky

Too vast to grab a single corner
So you stay like grass breaking siege by winter
Visible clouds like clothes
In constant change
Differ in decorations
You may dress up a possibility but not a sky
Slices of clouds resemble the footprints of a sage
Vague meaning behind his words
Visualized existence invites your imagination
You can guess what sky is all about
All your life's guesswork
Only gets you one side of a mirror
No way to get to the other side
And you are grass trying to break winter's siege
Staring into the empty color of blue or grey
Trying to understand and also be understood

6. 地

你踩坏了它的身体
它只会谅解
你可以做任何事情
可以依偎或呵斥或大喊
你更可以诉说
大地宽容　四季流换
这时你会无语　像土地一样沉实
有时你想把大地搬到身体内部
你只想体验
就像一位母亲体验分娩
你站在那儿只想替代大地
其实你哪儿都站不住
大地不留你　你只存在内心
所以　你说出了客观与主观的辩证
所以你走过大地时像一片叶子
没有值得怀念
大地也是一片叶子　你只看到它身上的几条纹路
是河流　也是皱纹

Land

You trampled her body
She can only forgive
You can almost do anything
Leaning on her, lamenting, yelling
And most of all talking
The ground is tolerant, with seasons running through
You wish for the grounded silence
Or to be inside its solid soil
An experience of a mother giving birth
You wish to stand in for the land, or become part of it
Only you can't demand to be rooted
The land is not taking you, you are only your inner world
So you talk about the subjective and objective dialectics
You talk about being a leaf to the land, insignificant to be remembered
The land is a leaf too, and you see only a few grains
They are rivers, and they are wrinkles

打开星星的光芒

7. 人

你永远是大地的努力
没有另一种人去欣赏你
在大地面前你只是黑色的蚂蚁
你的搬运只能维持某些理念
创造和毁灭是一条路途
你走着走着　会放牧生命的歌唱
你走着走着　也会看清大海是永远的滴泪
它挂在大地的一角　在你荒芜的眼角
使你的疑问不住地返回内心
你说　人哦　我叫不出你的名字来
你说着说着就沉默
就像你收藏的黑夜　那里正上演一幕幕梦境

Unveiling the Star's Light

Man

You forever drives the effort by the land
No other kind of man appreciates you
You are nothing but dark ants on the land
Moving about and transporting idealism
Creation and destruction happen on the same path
Singing carols as you continue your journey
And the ocean becomes a sea of tears
Hung in the corner of the land, deserted corner of the eye
Casting doubt onto yourself so you return to question
I can't tell who you are
A voice falling into a silenced hole
Like those dark nights you gathered
Bream scenes being replayed

8. 间

你说有多大就有多大
你说有多小就有多小
谁塞满了你的屋子
谁留驻了你的行程
又是谁大把大把地挥毫了你
这些不重要
就像世界在转　你也在转
世界空间有多大　你就有多大的房子或场所
因为你需要　空间混乱
比如　你在这里种上一个文字
就像小草　它的蔓延会造成拥挤
就像文字排列出的历史
那些文字空间　会再次让你安静下来
太阳之光　月色之光　涨满你的想象

Space

You can call out its size at will
Big, or small that fills up your room, stops your traveling
And one that contains you without restrain
But these are not important
As the earth and you keep on turning
Space is yours too, your space and home
Your needs, confused space
Like when you can plant a seed of words
Grass sprouts out and spreads into crowdedness
And words lay out history
Calm space between words
Light of the sun, shine from the moon
Permeating your imaginations

举起你的手来

这样好多了
我看见了风和周围的颜色
事物不动声色地走过
重生或死去
重要的是让我遇见一个过程
可以在那些遗迹里仰望手的高度

这是谁的一只手
天空通过四季卸下了重量
是否直抵你的内心
你举起来一直与谁保持着距离
很多时候我陷入你的光里靠近一座山
敲打石头　证明一种现象
很多时候我看着水中的倒影
把你反复模糊到太阳的眼前
想递进一种疼痛
看看你的样子是否影响了那些生命也弯一下腰
弯腰的时候　你的手上是否也生出露水的眼睛

而这是谁的一只手
在夜晚撒出星星的种子
种子的光植进土地
种子的光一夜间渗进城市的口袋　村庄的额头
让我与他们赶着梦　在你的意愿里走动
这样好多了
有一只手在头顶
我与他们在影子里坐北朝南　听一个海说着什么

打开星星的光芒

Raise Your Hand

This is better
Now I can see wind and colors nearby
Movements in silence
Rebirths or deaths
I see the process, the importance
I can look up and measure the height of raised hands
Among the relics

Whose hand is reaching way up high
As the sky unloads the seasons
Will the hand reach inside of you
Who does this distance keep you from, the raised hand
I stand in your light, closer to a mountain
I knock on the stone to prove an existence
Many times I look at the shadows in the water
Till you blur into the sunlight
I want to heighten a painful sensation
Seeing your face, how it changes lives as you bend
And when you bend, are there eyes of dew growing

Unveiling the Star's Light

In the palm of your raised hand

This hand belongs to you
Sowing seeds from the stars
Light of the seeds seeps into ground, seeping into
Pockets of cities, foreheads of farms
Chasing after dreams, following this lead
Swimming in desires, your wishes
This is a better choice – one hand above the heads
I'm sitting with them in the south corner facing north
Listening to the sound of the ocean

打开星星的光芒

你无法走进纯净的时间

你可以是任何一种形式
打掉灰尘　把名字放置一边
你可以把植物捆绑起来燃烧
坐在一块石头上思考
而你无法走进纯净的时间
你可以劫杀一滴水　在一粒沙子上奔跑
可以像黑夜兜起光来
还可以在一种声音里得到启示
把整个土地隐藏起来
可以在一朵云上变幻
而你无法走进纯净的时间

纯净的时间在一截朽死的木质体内
那是一种想
纯净的时间在星星的掩埋里
你在仰望的时候会感到撩目的疼
你会低下头来　怀疑起道路来

Unable to Enter Pure Time

You can by all means shake dust off, put your name aside
You can put plants in a bundle and burn them
You can sit still on a stone and meditate
But you cannot walk into pure time
You can kill a drop of water
Run on sand dunes
You can swaddle light in dark nights
Enlightened by a sound, putting the whole land under a tarp
Performing magic on a cloud
Yet you cannot touch pure time

Pure time resides inside a piece of aged wood
That is one theory
Pure time is buried inside stars
You can feel a sharp pain when you look up
Skeptical of the road ahead
When you return your gaze

打开星星的光芒

打开星星的光芒

这是谁走远时遗留的思考
这是谁把高远的思想安放在静里
是谁在聚炼大海与辽阔、早晨与黄昏的内涵
持久于凝重的形状,在风一次次催击时发出低吟
比鸟背负得持重,比云翻卷得彻底
而这是石头在沉静中与天空的对话

亿万年的对峙,石头说出天空的行走方式
石头在天空的书卷里找寻秘密的象形文字
如同星星的现场,替代了石头的未来
而谁又能聆听到对话的寓意
谁又能在一座大山中把一块块石头的心思验证
谁又能接近一道闪电抵达两者之间的内部
那些可能的话语是否还在世界上,被一场场雨解读

我只有在静的时候才打开天空
才打开隐秘的道路,才可以进入一朵花的过程
我可以忽略她白天的谎言,在一个深夜汲取她的唇

Unveiling the Star's Light

我知道花朵的真实只有在夜晚开放
只有在星星装满我的梦境之时
有一种声音撑起了花瓣,像我的睫毛
这些辽远的光辉,在我举头的默语中
已点燃眸子里的黑夜
在我接受世界之时,星星的光芒
以亘古的谜语呈现在大海撞击的礁石上
是谁隐秘的解释滴落在石头内部的光
那些撒满头顶的粮食、古老的词语
以一条河流的力量,冲刷着谁
就在我逢遇时间推敲的山顶
那些永久滞留的疑问,似乎漂着的沉重的石头
是哪些神圣的种子在播撒一种企愿
让我在面临黑暗时有一种冲动,说出最原始的温暖

说出最原始的光芒,打开星星
打开遗漏在沙砾上的光,打开沙漠上的光
打开一海涌动的光,打开土地上生长出故事的光
亿万年的积存下,我赤身走过
亿万年的点缀,我举着什么样的花环,面对空阔
我将要说出土地的脊背,读透自己的城市

打开星星的光芒

Unveiling the Star's Light

Who left reflections on a journey behind
Who put forth a sage's quest in silence
Who is distilling the ocean for its essence
A vast space blooming dawn and dusk with beauty
Holding a solid shape, humming in the wind
Heavier than the load on bird's wings
More thorough than how clouds turn over the sky
It is a composed dialogue between the stone and the sky

Billions of years in standoff, the stone knows the sky's moves
Searching for hieroglyphics in volumes of the sky
A scene of the stars, that's the stone's future
Who understands their dialogue
Who can tell what the rocks go through in a mountain
Who can approach the bolt of lightning to reach the inner worlds
Will those palpable words continue and be deciphered by storms

Only when it is quiet can I open the sky

Unveiling the Star's Light

Unblocking a hidden path, and entering a floral process
I can ignore their daytime lies and suck on her lips at night
The truth only blossoms in darkness
When stars fill up my dreams
A voice props up the petals, like my eye lashes
Glistening, upon my gazing silence
Lighting up the darkness in my eyes
When I accept the word, and hence the glory of the stars
Like ancient riddles displaying on the face of reefs
Whose mysterious interpretation sheds light inside a stone
Grain scatters over the heads like ancient words
Washing with the force of a river
As I encounter mountaintop formed in time
Those eternal quests, carrying the weight of stones
Sacred seeds spreading pledges
Rushing me to face the dark with a desire
Confession the most primitive warmth

For the most primitive lust, I unveil the stars
Setting free the light in sand, letting out the desert light
All the turbulent light, the light emitted through stories of the land
Formations of billions of years, I walk by them naked
Sparkles from a billion years ago, this majestic garland of light
Facing the vast sky
I shall speak the spine of the land and read into my city

打开星星的光芒

打开台灯,静静把世界放下来

是的,我是一枚走进你手中的苹果
感受自己体内宽大的秋天
那些神秘过程被灿烂包裹
那些被我感受到的就在一窗之外
今夜雨水丰盈
今夜,我会看见世界在雨里
那些归属的事物悄悄划过身旁
悄悄在我台灯的余光里

此时,我会静静把世界放下来
把高处的声音放下来,安顿远逝
此时,我会忘记自己,像一枚苹果
安静于内心
我沿着身体寻找一条沉静的水域
沉静的水域照见自己
呈现一次幸福
在台灯的余光里静默,被墙看见
我会在光里记下雨点的痕迹
记下一世界的重量

像累累的果实,缀满夜晚的枝头
充当另一群星星,照亮另一个世界

打开台灯,静静放下世界
这是幸福的时刻
默数一次心里的旅程
把自己看作一枚苹果,光芒的苹果与世界平静
这是任何声音无法进入的时刻
苹果饱满,苹果与台灯,还有雨中的世界
让我走进一幅古老的油画吧
今夜幸福,今夜贴在墙上

打开星星的光芒

Turn on the Lamp, and Turn off the World

Yes, I am an apple walking into your hand
Feeling the broad autumn days inside me
The mysterious process now surrounded by glory
Those feelings I once had are now in a window display
Tonight there is bountiful rain
Tonight, I shall see the world drenched
Those belongings glide quietly by
Glinting under my lamp

Now I shall quietly put down the world
Quieting lay down the voice from high above
Comforting those lost in faraway lands
Now I shall let go myself, like a fallen apple
Peace inside
I tread my body to search a tranquil water world
See my reflection in the dark
Display of temporary happiness
Meditating on the edge of the lamp, watched over by the wall
And I shall mark the traces of the rain

Take note of the feelings weighed by the world
Like abundant fruits hanging on the branches of the night
A cluster of stars, lighting up another world

Turn on the lamp, as I gently put down the world
This is a happy moment
Another journey counted for in silence
Seeing an apple, that is me, seeing it glow
And Peacefullness of the world
Such a moment impenetrable by any sound
Plump apple, apple and lamp, and the rainy world
I shall walk into this old vivid painting
Happiness is tonight, and tonight
In peace on the wall